Edmund Hobhouse

Sketch of the Life of Walter de Merton

SALZWASSER
VERLAG

Edmund Hobhouse

Sketch of the Life of Walter de Merton

Reprint of the original, first published in 1859.

1st Edition 2023 | ISBN: 978-3-37513-618-5

Verlag (Publisher): Salzwasser Verlag GmbH, Zeilweg 44, 60439 Frankfurt, Deutschland
Vertretungsberechtigt (Authorized to represent): E. Roepke, Zeilweg 44, 60439 Frankfurt, Deutschland
Druck (Print): Books on Demand GmbH, In de Tarpen 42, 22848 Norderstedt, Deutschland

SKETCH

OF THE

LIFE OF WALTER DE MERTON,

LORD HIGH CHANCELLOR OF ENGLAND, AND BISHOP OF ROCHESTER;
FOUNDER OF MERTON COLLEGE.

BY

EDMUND, BISHOP OF NELSON,

NEW ZEALAND;

LATE FELLOW OF MERTON COLLEGE, D.D.

Oxford and London:
JOHN HENRY AND JAMES PARKER.
1859.

PREFACE.

THE following memoir I have called a Sketch, for the sake of indicating my own estimate of its scantiness and incompleteness; and my chief aim in writing these prefatory words has been, (1.) to declare that a biography of Walter de Merton yet remains to be written; (2.) to express my hope that one of his own sons will gird himself to the work; and (3.) to point out what materials there are ready for the Merton biographer's hand.

It is with no small shame, as well as regret, that I bequeath to my possible successor an unfinished task, which I fully hoped that I should have been able to achieve myself with something of completeness.

It is more than ten years since I read the MS. memoirs of the founder by Dr. Francis Astrey, which Joseph Kilner has preserved to the college by transcription, and has both enlarged and corrected by notes and extracts from cotemporary documents. This memoir I reduced in bulk, believing that future researches in the Merton documents and into cotemporary history would bring to hand much additional matter; and the hope of adding this matter induced me to delay publication. The researches I have been able to make are not inconsiderable, as regards the number of documents examined, or the time spent in the process; but occasional failures of health and incessant occupation have made my antiquarian labours precarious, and the results scattered and unmethodized.

When, then, I found myself summoned to take charge of a New Zealand diocese, and consequently obliged to revise my laid-by work for publication, I was involved in the unexpected labour of verifying a large number of facts which had

turned up in the course of past researches; and to verify
which, fresh reference to a dark and unindexed muniment-
room was needed, or a fresh ramble amongst the numerous
and unarranged volumes of Kilner's transcript. The meagre-
ness of the subjoined Sketch is a result of the extreme
amount of time consumed in these verifications, and of the
consequent scantiness of time that could be secured, amidst
the pressing preparations for my impending change, for the
reconsideration of the whole work, and the hurried completion of its wanting chapters. Had not my worthy Pub-
lishers kindly offered the welcome facility of a piecemeal
issue in the monthly numbers of the "Gentleman's Maga-
zine," I doubt if I should ever have arrived at completion.

I will now state what materials there are available for
Walter de Merton's biography, and for a history of his college, which would be the appropriate sequel.

1. A MS. memoir by Dr. Francis Astrey (a Fellow early
in the eighteenth century, and a very laborious antiquary),
with Appendix, containing transcripts of original documents.
This memoir is written out by Kilner in his first MS. vol.,
and illustrated by him, after his manner, with divers extracts
written in margins, on blank pages, and between lines, and
often much perplexed by his comments and refutations.
This memoir may be taken to include all that is contained in
previous memoirs, of which the best is to be found in the
Latin Biographical Catalogue of Wardens and Fellows.

2. All the remaining volumes of Kilner's MSS., the
greater part consisting of transcripts from the evidences of
college estates. They contain also transcripts from Patent
and Close Rolls, then unprinted; extracts from Rymer's *Fœdera*, the *Textus Roffensis*, Antony Wood's works, and other
antiquarian repertories. There is also some original matter;
e. g., on the founder's kindred, on the rise of the aularian and
collegiate systems, on corporate seals, on the king's courts, &c.,

and all manifesting an immense range of reading and research and an unflinching labour, but unhappily marred by great perplexity of style and a great want of arrangement and indexing.

3. Kilner's "Pythagoras' School," printed (not published) about 1790, to correct the misstatements of a paper which appeared in Grose's "Antiquities," on the subject of the ancient Norman building which the founder bought in Cambridge, in 1270, of the family of Fitz-Eustace, or Dunning, and which had been invested by Cambridge antiquaries with the absurd name of Pythagoras' School. In this treatise he proceeds to give some very valuable information respecting the earliest college foundations of Oxford and Cambridge, and then adds 150 pages of "Something Supplementary," containing seven distinct heads. These treatises are short, and from their style almost unintelligible, but they are rendered exceedingly valuable by the profuse annexation of original documents, including the principal charters of the college, the founder's will, executors' accounts[a], &c., copied with singular correctness.

This valuable bequest to his college would have been without drawback had there been any arrangement of the documents, or index, to aid the frequent references which so rich a repertory tempts the historian to make. A copy of this book I placed in the college library in 1842.

4. Cotemporary documents generally, including the charters, deeds relating to purchase and conveyance of estates, the successive issue of statutes, the founder's will, and executors' accounts. Most of these are to be found, somewhere or other, in Kilner's[b] printed or unprinted volumes.

---

[a] He has also given some engravings of the early seals of founders and benefactors, found in the Merton exchequer. An index to the original documents printed in this book would be a great acquisition.

[b] Or in Baker's Transcripts of Evidences. Baker was employed by the college, *circa* 1670-80, to transcribe in the muniment-room. The result was an enormous

5. Rymer's *Fœdera*, the Close and Patent Rolls, Prynne's
" Records," the *Rotuli Hundredorum*, and the *Inquisitiones post
Mortem*, though largely used by Astrey and Kilner, and partially searched by myself, would probably still yield some
fresh facts relating to the founder of Merton, or to the persons with whom, or to the circumstances with which, he was
concerned.

6. I must not omit to lay upon the Merton biographer
the duty of making himself much better acquainted than I am
with the political, academic, and ecclesiastical history of the
times; and I feel safe in promising him that such an ac-
quaintance will reward him by enabling him to present to
himself and the public Walter de Merton's true historical
place, and the exact designs of his institution °, and of its
peculiar form and provisions ; all which, I am satisfied, are
yet insufficiently un derstood.

I doubt not, too, that a study of the cotemporary history
of the foreign Universities, especially that of Paris, then
holding very close literary commerce with Oxford, will
throw some light on the origin and purpose of some of the
Merton provisions.

I will now mention that I had it in my mind, and I hope
I may bequeath my intention to some worthy legatee of my
college kindred, to add a chapter relating the sad history

---

volume of costly parchment, containing the evidences of Ponteland, Emildon, and
one or two other estates, but so ignorantly done as to necessitate collation with
the originals.

* I would instance specially its relation to the conventual institutions, and particularly the friars, then possessed of the chief scholastic strongholds in the two
Universities. I will here acknowledge my debt to Mr. Brewer's *Monumenta
Franciscana*, consisting mainly of the letters of Adam de Marisco, the Franciscan
reader in Oxford, and the great friend of Bishop Grostete of Lincoln, and exhibiting very strikingly the amazing amount of influence, ecclesiastical and political,
which accrued to the friars from their successful seizure of the seats of learning.
It appears that Walter de Merton carried a commendatory letter from this cele-
brated reader, on the occasion of his going to Bishop Grostete for sub-deacon's
orders ; but unhappily the letter has no date.

of the founder's little hospital of St. John, Basingstoke [d], his first eleemosynary creation; and that for this end I examined a large mass of Basingstoke evidences and bailiffs' rolls, of which an abstract will be found in the Basingstoke box in thé muniment-room. Further, I designed to devote a chapter to the college in its completed condition, endeavouring to present to the mind the young *familia Mertonensis* in its first stage of life, 1274—1288; and another chapter to its first century of existence, up to the time of the addition of Wyllyot's *Portionistœ*.

I will now subjoin a specification, though not very exact, of the classes of documents which the Merton muniment-room contains, hoping that an introduction of this kind may serve to mitigate the dread which the first sight of their number and want of order tends to inspire in the would-be historical inquirer.

I. Those which affect the being or well-being of the corporate life :—Charters and confirmations, statutes, interpretations, injunctions, licenses of mortmain, pardons, exemptions.

II. Those which affect title to property [e] :—Impropriations, grants, and conveyances to the founder or his college

---

[d] This institution, having a most slender provision for its purpose, the founder annexed to his college for its government, and commended it in his statutes, for its better endowment, to the grateful bounty of those individual beneficiaries of his foundation whom Providence should bless with increased means. The result was, that within a few years of his death the hospital estate was farmed like any other, with the exception of the lessee's undertaking to maintain the chapel-services ; all eleemosynary purpose seems to have been forgotten, and at the dissolution the estate passed to the Court of Augmentations, from whence it was restored to the college by Edward VI., and finally, all remnants of the chapel disappeared in the eighteenth century.

[e] The old arrangement of these was in separate oaken boxes and in several bundles within the box, each bundle distinguished by a coloured letter, and each deed by a figure. Thus A. Wood quotes from *Pyx. Oxon. A. ruber.* 37, &c., &c. The present drawers were made in 1842, and the deeds only *partially* transferred to them. The drawers contain not only evidences, but a medley of leases, bailiffs' rolls, court rolls, and bursarial papers.

of estates with previous title-deeds, (some of these of early Norman times,) legal proceedings affecting title.

III. Those which relate to the internal management of the corporate affairs :—Registers of college acts, from 1482, begun by Warden Fitzjames, with preface, setting forth the inconvenience of having no record of acts [1]. Bursars' rolls; these are now arranged according to reigns, in pigeon-holes, from Elizabeth's time; they are written out in *Libri Bursariorum*. Riding bursars' rolls; accounts of journeys to the northern estates. Wardens' rolls, not numerous, but the warden was required to account to the college, *per billam*, for all moneys collected by him or dispensed. Sub-wardens' rolls, often intitled *Rotuli Depositariorum;* they digested in one sheet the receipts of the three bursars of the year under the head of each estate. Chaplains' rolls; in the early period the chaplains were, as the founder intended, men whose years, experience, and gravity gave them influence in the college: several of them, in Edward I., II., and III.'s time, were entrusted with the laying out of large sums for the college *in officio procuratoris*, as it was sometimes called, but most especially on the chapel buildings. Catalogues of fellows; it is said that no catalogue was made till the time of Edward IV.; the oldest now existing is that formed by Sir Henry Savile, but as the names of a large proportion of the fellows appear in the bursars' rolls as *senescalli septimanæ*, or stewards of the fellows' table, he had large access to documentary proof. This, however, fails in the case of more than one of a sur-

---

[1] An old book bound in rough calf nevertheless exists, (quoted by A. Wood as *quoddam vetus registrum*,) containing some detached entries of college acts, leases, &c., of the fifteenth century and earlier, on parchments of various sizes and dates. This greatly needs indexing. The old (Fitzjames's) register is not completely indexed. A pretty full abstract of the earlier portion was made, in 1839, by Dr. J. R. Hope, and is valuable. The same accurate investigator left a valuable compilation to this room in the form of a *corpus statutorium*, or body of statutory and disciplinary documents, gathered from Lambeth registers, college registers, and visitatorial proceedings.

name, the Christian name not being given : hence we are unable to prove that the " Wyclif" who appears as *senescallus* temp. Edward III. was the famous reformer John, or a cotemporary. Savile claims him, but offers no evidence.

IV. Those which relate to the management of estates :— Court-rolls ; a large mass of these are rolled up in the boxes, and have never been examined ; some of the later ones have been bound. Bailiffs' rolls ; very voluminous, but here and there rewarding search by very interesting facts and customs. The whole property was at first managed by the agency of bailiffs, as contemplated by the statutes. *Rentalia*, chiefly *in villâ* Oxon, of the house property. Leases ; some very ancient ones exist, but the system of leasing entire estates did not supersede that of bailiff-management until the end of the fifteenth century. The oldest register contains leases, as well as all other college documents ; but lease-books were established in Elizabeth's reign, and are all extant. Terriers, surveys, maps.

V. Miscellaneous :—Transcripts of original documents. Indexes, of which the *Liber Ruber* is the most remarkable. It is an index of the documents of the muniment-room in 1288, unhappily stripped of its red cover, bound in parchment, and misnamed *Registrum*. The great want of the muniment-room at this moment is a *Liber Ruber* of its present contents. I have indexed the boxes containing the Basingstoke, Thorncroft, and St. John's parish evidences, but no more. The old *Liber* forms a basis, for it is still a correct index of the most ancient evidences. There is a transcript of the whole, in more legible hand, and a partial one in Antony Wood's box.

CONTENTS.

DEDICATION.

MY DEAR WARDEN,

Before this reaches you, the relation which has subsisted between us as Warden and Fellow for more than seventeen years will have ceased.

There is only one act by which I can now testify my respect for your person and office, and that is the request I now make, that you will kindly accept the dedication of the following Sketch of our honoured Founder's Life. This I must beg you to do with great forbearance towards the execution of the work, which falls far short of what your reverence for the Founder's character would bid you desire. I heartily regret that I have failed in producing anything worthier of your acceptance and of his memory. I could have wished that my Merton life had been prolonged if only I could have rendered, in this and other respects, some worthier return than I have for the manifold advantages received, But I must now comfort myself with thinking that the life now opening before me is one which is most strictly in keeping with our Founder's intentions as to the ultimate destination of the beneficiaries of his institution; for he fully intended (herein differencing his college from the religious bodies which bound their members to conventual duties for life) that his scholars should carry forth, " in profectum Ecclesiæ," the blessings of Christian truth and discipline from the walls where he had nurtured them for awhile in godliness and good learning; nor was the mission-field either absent from his mind or alien from his purpose. The recovery of the lost domains of Christendom was the only form in which the high Christian duty of the propagation of the Gospel presented itself as feasible; and in this form our Founder shewed his readiness to embrace and fulfil that duty. In his statutes he allows his college to contract the number of fellowships, on account of a " subsidium terræ sanctæ;" in his will he left a bequest for the purpose of sending a " bonus vir" to the crusades. Such zeal for the propagation of the faith, had it lived in the nineteenth instead of the thirteenth century, would have rejoiced in the extension of our Colonial Churches, and the continual enlargement of the missionary field by conquests far less costly and far more fruitful than our Founder's legatee was ever destined to witness. I feel, then, that in my mission to New Zealand I have not only Walter de Merton's God's speed, as fully as his "bonus vir" could have had in donning his armour for the Holy Land, but that I am acting most fully in the spirit of the Founder, and of the purposes of his institution, as a handmaid to the Church, in going forth to endeavour to lay the foundations of a new episcopate in a land which is one of the most recent conquests of the faith, now, henceforth, and for ever, I trust, to be reckoned amongst the kingdoms of Christ.

Ever, my dear Warden,

Yours, with most affectionate and dutiful respect,

EDMUND NELSON.

MALTA, EN ROUTE TO NEW ZEALAND,
DEC. 22, 1858.

SKETCH OF THE LIFE OF WALTER DE MERTON,

FOUNDER OF MERTON COLLEGE, OXFORD.

CHAPTER I.

THE EARLY LIFE, UP TO THE FOUNDATION OF THE COLLEGE.

THE earliest documentary evidence extant connects the founder of Merton College, through property and through blood, with the town of Basingstoke. In that town certainly lay the inheritance of his mother and of her numerous kindred, the Heriards[a], Olivers, Fitz-aces; and there, probably, her son grew up, amongst those neighbours who, in their still extant conveyances, delight to call the rising *clericus* by such affectionate titles as *dilectum socium et amicum*. No surname is ever attached to the father, whose Christian name was William. We have, therefore, no ground for supposing that he had any tie with Merton as a birthplace or residence. And out of what connection the name of *de Merton*, by which his son is invariably described, arose, whether through birth, or education at the Priory[b], does not now appear.

Merton[c], I know not on what certain evidence, is always stated to have been the birthplace of Walter. All that is certain is, that his name was acquired from the priory;—see in his statutes, 1264, § 19:—"Domui insuper de Merton, a quâ nomen sortiuntur, grati semper sint et eam, utpote hujus operis adjutricem studeant adjuvare."

1237-8. The first document relating to the founder gives an unusual insight into the family history. It is a Close Roll of the 22nd Henry III., (*in dorso m. 14, et inde habet cartam regis,*)

---

[a] Heriard is a village near Basingstoke. Edmond de Heriard, I find, was Prior of Merton in 1296. See Dugdale's *Monasticon*. A Heriard was one of the King's Justices under Kings Richard and John. See Madox, "Bar. Ang.," 233.

[b] A priory of Austin Canons founded *circa* 1125 by Henry I. and Gilbert Norman. Hugh de Basyng was Prior 1231-8, probably a Hampshire neighbour of the founder's. He was followed by Gilbert de Ashe, another Hampshire name. Merton, Malden, and Chessington are adjoining villages in Surrey, near Kingston.

[c] Walter had kindred settled in the neighbourhood of Merton, e.g., Peter de Codynton, through whose patronage he became Rector of Codynton.

entitled, "Inquisitio de Terris Walteri de Merton in Manerio [d] de Basingstoke," and describes an inquiry held, it appears, at his instance, in consequence of his being overcharged by the king's bailiff. The jury present, that Walter's property consists of one virgate and a-half, and ten acres of land, and two tenants; the whole subject to 10s. 4d., payable to the manor of Basingstoke: that it was given by John Fitz-ace to his niece Cristina till her uncle's death, when it fell into the king's hands, and was given by him to William, (a cousin of Richard de Heriet,) who married Cristina: and that William and Cristina demised it to Walter, their son and heir, (then called *clericus,* but with no preferment.)   They present also, that Walter had acquired some small parcels of property from Robertus de Basinges [e], Walter fil. Alexandri, and Rob. de Waltham.

The king remits all demands, and fixes his future payments for all his property within the manor at 15s. per annum, *pro omni servitio.*

Walter is here styled *clericus,* but without any specified preferment.   He had probably addicted himself to the study of law in London, and was earning both money and influence by the exercise of his talents in that profession. For in the conveyance of Rob. de Waltham, mentioned in the Inquisition, it is bargained, that Walter, besides paying 50s., is to place the seller " cum quadam summâ pecuniæ in aliquo servitio vel ad aliquod officium addiscendum apud London aut alibi," before the feast of All Saints, 25th Hen. III., (Nov. 1, 1240).

With regard to his education nothing certain is known.   He is said to have studied firstly at the Priory of Merton, and then at Oxford; and both are more than probable. Ingram ("Memorials of Oxford," vol. i. p. 3) asserts the tradition that he was an inmate of Mauger Hall, now the Cross Inn, in the Cornmarket [f].

To return to certainty. His parents were both buried at Basingstoke, in the parish church of St. Michael. Cristina died first, and it was probably in the recent grief for her loss that he pro-

---

[d] A manor in *manu regis.*

[e] The conveyance of these small parcels are in the Merton exchequer, with several others, all undated. See transcripts in Kilner's Appendix.

[f] Vid. infra, p. 19. The introduction of the young candidate for the subdeaconship by the Oxford Franciscan reader makes it highly probable that he had been a pupil of that eminent teacher in Oxford. I much regret that I can find no clue to the date of this letter, and that I was unacquainted with its existence till after the publication of this chapter.

ceeded to devote the house [f] which he inherited from her to the charitable purpose of a hospital [h], "ad sustentationem pauperum Christi transeuntium," "pro salute animæ meæ, et laudabilis conversationis mulieris Cristinæ matris meæ, de consensu et voluntate Domini et patris mei."

The exact date of this deed of endowment does not appear, but it seems to have been very shortly superseded by a second, consequent upon the death of his father. They are both witnessed by exactly the same persons and in the same order; in both the founder is called simply *clericus*, and I hence infer that they are very near each other in time.

The second deed conveys a somewhat larger endowment than the first [i]; it adds the whole *tenementum*, or holding, late William Cok's, to his house, which, in consequence of the first deed, had been known as *Mansum S[i] Joannis.* It was to embrace a larger scope of charity,—the support of ministers of the altar, "ad egestatem et imbecillitatem vergentium," as well as of the poor travellers. The brethren of the hospital were to hold of him and his heirs, *tanquam patroni*, in pure alms; subject only to the maintenance of two wax lights at St. Mary's altar in Basingstoke Church, which lights his parents had habitually offered there.

There is no mention of a chapel attached to the hospital. Indeed, the institution must have been on the very humblest scale, commencing with no endowment but that of a single house, and dependent on the voluntary services of brethren, and on the alms of the neighbours. But it seems to have become at once an object of general regard amongst his fellow-townsmen, for the deeds about this time are numerous which convey small parcels of land to the brethren and *sisters* of St. John. We may presume that the donations of other than real property were still more frequent.

To continue the history of this hospital. The founder did not spare his growing interest in high quarters to advance his cherished undertaking. In the 37th Hen. III., June 25, 1253, the king at Suwick (qy. Southwick) grants to the master and brethren to have

---

[f] "Mansum quod quandam Will[e] le Cok tenuit de antecessoribus meis."

[h] His dedication is, "Deo et gloriosæ Virgini Mariæ genetrici suæ, et venerabili Patrono meo S. Joanni Bapt."

[i] It also adds, "pro salute Reverendi Dñi mei, Dñi Henrici Regis." Does this imply the enjoyment of the royal patronage?

a chantry in the hospital chapel; and July 8, 1253, the founder got a confirmation of his last endowment from the king at Portsmouth. In 1262 (July 8), the king at Canterbury, surrounded by his chief statesmen, in a deed commencing with an inflated preamble on the duty of keeping the clergy from poverty, makes the hospital of St. John a royal foundation for the support of needy clergy, "et pauperum ibidem infirmantium." The fruits of this royal patronage were the enjoyment of a free chapel and freedom from all secular service. The founder is here styled *clericus,* and *familiaris noster,* and also *canonicus Wellensis.*

In 1268, the freedom of the chapel, of its services and oblations, was secured by the highest ecclesiastical authority. The deed of Cardinal Ottobon, the papal legate, securing this freedom, is in good preservation in the Exchequer, in duplicate, with perfect seal.

The future history of this hospital belongs rather to that of the college than of the founder of Merton. We must now return to his personal history.

By the Inquisition above named we learn that the founder was in holy orders in 1238. In 1249, in a grant of free-warren within the demesne lands of Malden, adjoining the parish of Merton, he is styled by the king *clericus noster,* which probably means either that he was a chaplain, or that he practised in the king's courts. He must by this time either have had good preferment, or the more profitable employment [k] of a canonist, or both, as he declares that he acquired these lands by his own industry, (Stat. Coll. Mert., cap. i.)

He certainly obtained preferment [l] from Nicholas de Farnham (his countryman), Bishop of Durham 1241—1248; but as we have evidence of his treating for the lands of Malden, &c., as early as

---

[k] See *Registrum Ant. Brevium,* in Bibl. Cotton. f. 199. Walter is mentioned as *Prothonotarium Cancellariæ,* in which capacity he framed some useful writs. The fees of this office were considerable; e.g. Anno Iº. Joannis, one mark of gold for the Chancellor, one silver for the Vice-Chancellor, one silver for the Prothonotary. See Kilner's Astrey MS., p. 14.

[l] The rectory of Sedgefield, co. of Durham, he held till his death. See his will, wherein he disposed of the profits of that rectory accruing after his consecration. He also bequeathed to the poor of Staindrop, co. of Durham, twenty marks, and likewise to the poor of other places where he held preferment, with bequests to monks at Newcastle and Hartlepool. He recounts this bishop amongst other benefactors for whose souls his first college at Malden was meant to intercede. Of Nicholas Farnham's learning, see A. Wood's "Annals," 1229.

24 Hen. III., 1240, he must have found other means of making his industry profitable.

The documents relating to his acquisition of the Surrey estates, Malden, Farleigh, Chessington, (and later), Thorncroft and Leatherhead, are very complete, and they shew the complicated dealings, which the feudal tenure made necessary for the conveyance of land, especially of such as was to be placed in mortmain.

The advowson of Malden with Chessington was granted to him by the Priory of Merton; that of Farleigh, by the Priory of Tortington, Sussex.

1254. In 1254 or 5 we have evidence of his being Chancellor, or holding some office that gave him at a distance the reputation of being Chancellor. It is derived from letters [m] from the Bishops of St. Andrew's and Glasgow in behalf of Nicholas Corbet, the king of Scots' kinsman, a Scotch suitor in Chancery, in which Walter is called *Cancellarius Regis.* As he was prothonotary (see supra), he might, by the Scotch bishops, have been mistaken for the superior officer; perhaps he held the office for a very short time, for in 1256, in a grant from the king of some land at Basingstoke, he is styled simply *clericus noster.*

In 1257 he appears as witness to a charter, in company with others of the king's council.

In 1258[n], May 6, he was certainly entrusted with the great seal, and left by the king, when he withdrew himself from London, to settle with the pope's legate the grant of the kingdom of Sicily from the pope to Edmund, Earl of Lancaster, the king's son, and to set the seal to any letters or powers relating thereto [o].

In 1259[p], June 15, the king presented him to the prebend of Cantler's, or Kentish Town, in St. Paul's (*sede vacante*): this was

---

[m] Rymer's *Fœdera*, tom. i. p. 570, transcribed by Kilner, App. No. IV. p. 64. Henry Wengham succeeded W. de Kilkenny in the chancellorship on the eve of Epiphany, 39th Hen. III., Jan. 5, 1255. Pat. Rolls, m. 15.

[n] Cal. Rol. Pat. 42nd Hen. III. "Sept°. Maii, morabatur Hen. de Wengham London' infirmus, et sigillum remansit penes Dñum Wm. de Merton." See Chron. T. Wikes, p. 55.

[o] 1258. Pat. Rol. Hen. III. 42, m. 2. There is an Act of the King in Council touching the dependence of advowsons upon manors :—"Teste Rege per Consil Regis pro negotio Walteri de Merton, 14 marks." See Kennett's Case of Appropriations, Append., No. V.

[p] In the 44th Hen. III., 1259—60, two Chancery records occur, issued "de ordinatione Walteri de Merton."—*Prynne's Coll.*, p. 96, transcribed by Kilner.

soon after exchanged for that of Holywell, now called Finsbury, in the same Church.

On July 4 he was collated by the Bishop of Exeter to a prebend in that church.

In 1260 he was Chancellor, but was soon removed by the barons; but in 1261[q], while the Court kept Whitsuntide at Winchester, the king restored him, (as Matthew of Westminster declares, *inconsulto baronagio*,) with cccc.[r] marks per annum; and in 1261-2, Jan. 29, he is joined with Philip Basset, the Chief-Justice; and Robert Walerand, to treat with three deputies of the disaffected barons, and to report to Richard, king of the Romans, the king's brother, as referee of the disputed points[s]. Both these names are of great interest to the sons of Merton; the first as a great patron of the founder, and the second as the husband of the pious Ela Comitissa, to whom they owe one of their oldest benefactions, the manor of Thorncroft, in Leatherhead. See Wood's " Hist. and Antiq.," lib. ii. pp. 85-6.

His preferments still continued to grow, for the king, who was sore pressed for money, (as appears by a letter, translated from Tower Rolls, of Sept. 12, 1262,) had no mode of paying him so ready[t]. He presented him in this year[u] to the church of Preston in Anderness, Lancashire, and to the prebend of Yatesbury, in Sarum.

The king was now in France, and in a very forlorn plight. His Chancellor, whom he left in England, must consequently have had

---

[q] Prynne gives two letters addressed to Walter de Merton as Chancellor, 45th Hen. III., translated by Kilner; and Kilner, Astrey's Memoir, p. 9, transcribes, from the Close Rolls 46th Hen. III., m. 4, two letters from the King to the Chancellor, Aug. 18 and Sept. 12, 1262, and from Rymer's MSS. Collectanea one from Richard, king of the Romans, to the Chancellor, "amico nostro carissimo," June 16, 1262.

[r] Liberate Rolls, 45th Hen. III., *ad sustentationem sui et Cancellariæ nostræ.* 15th Oct., 1261.

A.D. 1261. T. Wikes:—"Hoc Ann. Dñs W⁵. de Merton factus est custos regii sigilli."

[s] The letter of Richard, king of the Romans, declaring the failure of this reference, is given by Rymer, tom. i. pp. 738, 9; Kilner, p. 132. He speaks of the founder as then Chancellor.

[t] The profuse bestowal of Church patronage was the common mode of rewarding the clerical servants of the crown; witness John Mansel, the king's principal favourite, who is said to have had the largest Church revenues of any dignitary less than a bishop in any age. (Kilner.) He was Lord Keeper in 1247, and again in 1249. (Beatson.)

[u] June 20. Vid. Patent Rolls, Hen. III., m. 9; transcribed by Kilner, MS. Memoir, p. 10.

the chief burden of a troubled and ill-governed kingdom lying upon him. There is a letter[x] from John Mansel, the king's secretary, written from Paris in 1262, in which he speaks of the king being near Rheims, with very few of his own people about him, and bent on making a progress through Burgundy. He begs for the Chancellor's commands, and a report on the state of the kingdom, (Rymer's *Fœd.*, i. 752.) From hence we learn that the king was not only absent, but ignorant of his kingdom's affairs, and that even his secretary was looking to the Chancellor at home for commands. It was probably during this trying period that the Chancellor's character most fully shone forth, and that he earned the high opinion which, it is plain, the whole of the royal family entertained of him,—witness the fact of their all contributing in some way to the foundation of his college.

In 1263, June 29th, the Bishop of Worcester (Cantilupe) wrote to him, begging him to persuade the king to accept the barons' terms; in which entreaty he probably succeeded[y], as a short peace ensued. In the same year he had the more difficult task laid upon him of procuring money for Robert de Nevill, whom the king had placed in command in the counties beyond Trent, (Rymer, i. p. 772,) to hold them against the rebels. Later in this year, (Sept. 18,) the king retired again from England, and left the seal in the keeping of Nicolas de Ely[z], from whom the barons had before obtained it. Perhaps this was a toward dispensation for our founder, who was less prominent as an object of attack in the riots which ensued in Lent, 1264, in London and elsewhere, and in which his prebendal house at Finsbury was plundered. This violence produced a letter[a]

---

[x] Pat. 46 Hen. III., m. 7. Rymer gives three letters, addressed to Walter de Merton as Chancellor in 1262 and 1263; viz., from J. Mansel, tom. i. p. 752; from the Bishop of Exeter, tom. i. p. 758, March 9, 1262-3; from the Bishop of Worcester, tom. i. p. 768, June 29, 1263.

[y] 4th of July. The King commissioned the Bishops of London, Lincoln, Lichfield, and two laymen to treat with the barons. See Pat. 47 Hen. III., m. 7.

[z] Rymer, tom. i. p. 775; see also *Anglia Sacra,* vol. iv. p. 496. An agreement between the King and barons to refer their differences to the award of the King of France was sealed at Windsor, Dec. 16. The award followed in Jan. 22, 1263-4, but led to greater outrage on the barons' part against the King's adhèrents.

[a] Two letters of the King,—Jan. 12, 1263-4, Pat. 48 Hen. III., m. 3; Aug. 9, 1264, Claus. 48 Hen. III., m. 4,—are transcribed in Kilner's MS., pp. 12 and 14; the first giving him a warrant of chase in any royal forest he might pass through; the second to the mayor of London, enjoining protection to the founder's prebendal estate, at the request of the Bishops of London, Worcester, Sarum, Winton, Exeter, Chichester, and others.

from the king to the mayor of London, enjoining him forthwith to rescue the late Chancellor's property.

His release from office gave him leisure for other thoughts and other business, more in keeping with his sacred character. The king, being in this interval wholly under the power of the barons, obtained from them letters of safeguard protecting the ex-Chancellor while keeping residence at his various preferments. This was a service of no slight danger, as it involved travelling from Durham to Lancashire, Exeter, Salisbury, and St. Paul's. This letter[b] was of course in the king's name, but *de Consilio Baronum,* which shews in whose power he was. Nevertheless, we may suppose that he gladly obtained any measure of safety for his faithful servant; and certainly the founder's beneficiaries owe a debt of gratitude for the repose thus obtained, which he employed in ripening his plans for the foundation of the house on the manor of Malden, and in drawing up statutes for its regulation. This *Ordinatio* is dated in 1264, but has no month assigned to it. In the statutes of 1270 it is spoken of as having been executed *tempore turbationis Angliæ,* but as the baronial war went on unappeased through the whole of that year and the following, until the battle of Evesham, Aug. 4, it is beyond our power to give any more exact date.

---

[b] Pat. 48th Hen. III., m. 12, printed in Prynne's Records, vol. ii. p. 1006. " *Omnibus, &c. salutem.*—Cum de consilio Baronum nostrorum providerimus, quod clerici ecclesiarum rectores, vicarii, &c. personæ ecclesiasticæ apud beneficia sua ecclesiastica personalem facere volentes residentiam, salvo et secure et absque impedimento nostri vel nostrorum in beneficiis suis valeant commorari, ac dilectus clericus noster Walterus de Merton, sicut intelleximus, residentiam hujusmodi apud beneficia sua quæ obtinet in Regno nostro facere proponet. Vobis mandamus quod eidem Waltero in eundo vel redeundo seu moram faciendo apud beneficia sua prædicta nullum inferatis, vel quantum in vobis est inferri permittatis dampnum, impedimentum, injuriam seu gravamen. In cujus, &c.''

CHAPTER II.

THE FOUNDATION OF HIS COLLEGE.

THESE facts are certain with regard to the foundation of the college.

1. That the charter of incorporation with the first body of statutes was obtained in 1264. (In Rot. Cartar. 48th Henry III., m. 2.)

2. That this foundation was the development of a previous one of unknown date.

3. That the Society was established in the manor of Malden, but in connection with the University of Oxford.

The Charter Roll is to be found in the Charter Rolls of 48th Henry III., m. 2. It is much to be noted as the first incorporation of any body of persons for purposes of *study* in this kingdom, and as the first effort to raise the condition of the secular clergy by bringing them into close connection with an academical course of study.

But it was not the primary form which the founder's intentions had taken.

There is a document existing amongst the Malden title-deeds containing an assignation of that manor, with Chessington and Farley, for the sustentation of John de la Clythe and seven other *nepotes*, all recited by name, who were called "scolares in scolis degentes," stated to be living under an *ordinatio* approved by the king, by the feudal lord, and by the Bishop of Winchester and his chapter. This assignation bears no date, and there is some difficulty in fixing one, for the only personage mentioned is the Bishop of Winchester, designated only by the initial "J," and this initial ties the document to some date posterior to Oct. 18, 1262, when John of Exeter was nominated by the pope to that see, after a vacancy of two years, owing to a disputed election upon the death of Aymer de Lusignan.

But that a settlement of the estates upon certain *scholares*, and that an *ordinatio* for this purpose existed somewhat earlier, we learn from a charter of Richard, Earl of Gloucester [*], May 7, 1262,

---

[*] Printed by Kilner, p. 51.

empowering the founder to assign his manor to the priory of Merton, or other religious house, for the sustenance of "clerici in scolis degentes," according to the founder's *ordinatio,* or any future one he should think fit to establish.

It was to be expected that the founder's intention revealed by this charter, of vesting his estates in a religious house as a trustee for his scholastic design, would have manifested itself in the deed of assignation, were that deed a posterior document. But if the dates given by Le Neve, relating to the appointment of Bishop J.—— of Winchester, are correct, the Earl's charter must have been executed in the month of May *preceding* the Bishop's consecration, which, on the authority of the *Chronicon Dovorense,* is placed by Le Neve a little before Michaelmas.

The only conclusion to which we can come is, that the founder had in his mind the project of vesting his estates in the hands of an existing religious corporation; that he took powers from his feudal lord for that purpose [d]; that for some reason or other he did not execute this project, and that he contented himself with assigning the manors to his nephews under an ordinance sanctioned by such authority in Church and State as he could procure [e].

The description of the founder, *quondam Cancellarius,* is the next chronological help to which we must turn [f]. Several letters addressed to the founder as Chancellor, in 1262 and 1263, are still extant, which leave little doubt that he held the office continuously up to June 29, 1263, when Bishop (Cantilupe) of Worcester wrote beseeching him to induce the king to try the effect of mediation for the pacification of the barons.

In September following we know that the great seal had, by the resolution of the barons, devolved upon Nicolas, Archdeacon of Ely, for the term [g] of the king's absence from England.

[d] These powers he did not previously possess. The earlier conveyances from the mesne lords, de Watevile and Codynton, and the confirmations by the chief lord, the Earl of Gloucester, bar the right of assigning " Judæis et domibus religiosis."

[e] The instrument looks very much like one published in a manorial court. The names of the witnesses seem local and humble.

[f] From John Mansell, 46th Henry III., no month; the Bishop of Exeter, 47th Henry III., feast of St. Gregory, probably March 12, 1262-3 ; Bishop of Worcester, June 29, 1263; Lord Neville, no month. See Rymer, t. i. pp. 752, 758, 768, 772.

[g] The king left Westminster with intent to cross the sea, Sept. 18. By an order, Dec. 18, the barons decreed that the seal should continue in Nicolas de Ely's hands as long as the king remained abroad. Rymer's *Fœd.,* tom. i. p. 775; *Anglia Sacra,* vol. i. p. 496.

Somewhere then about this period, September, 1263, the *quondam Cancellarius* must be supposed to have published his deed of assignment to his nephews, so soon to be superseded by the charter of incorporation obtained in the course of the ensuing year.

Assuming then that the power acquired for the De Clares to convey the Malden estate to religious houses was never acted upon, the document (which I assign to 1263, *circa* Sept.) gives us the earliest stage of the founder's benevolent intentions. It presents to us a family arrangement, placing eight of his nephews, under a warden and chaplains, in his manor-house, with a lifelong provision; entitling them "*scolares in scolis degentes*;" and tying them to a life of study and of rule, for they were to forfeit their places should they disregard the *ordinatio*, or commit any serious offence.

This assignment, it should be remarked, though it lacked the force of incorporation, was intended to be perpetual in its benefits to the recipients. The vacancies were to be filled up by *consanguinei*, or others, the nomination of whom the founder reserved to himself. But as a legal disposition of property, the founder could hardly have regarded it as final. Indeed, it is not easy to see in whom the legal estate at that time was vested; and as the *ordinatio* [h] is lost, we can get no light from that document, which probably would have given some indirect information.

Some security for sustaining the assignment of the property in its charitable purposes was, no doubt, secured from the powerful patronage under which it was effected. Besides the approval of the monarch and of the diocesan given to the *ordinatio*, the founder was able to secure the patronage of the Earls of Gloucester, which implied some effective lay power for keeping the beneficiaries to an observance of their duties.

We find Earl Richard commending the institution to the protection of his successors, "suæ defensionis clypeo perpetuo contuendam;" adding, "Qui etiam (i. e. his successors) supra ipsos ad quos dicta maneria ex ordinatione supradictâ devenerunt, liberum et plenam habeant potestatem ipsos compellandi per potestatem secularem ad observationem ordinationis supradictæ."

---

[h] I regret to find that no copy of this *ordinatio* exists in the archives of the see or the chapter of Winchester. No episcopal register is extant earlier than John de Pontissara's episcopate, 1282, and there are no capitular documents relating to Merton except those which affect patronage of livings.

The latter power is dropped in the charter of his son Gilbert in 1264, when the revised *ordinatio* had placed the patronage in the diocesan, and, by virtue of its force as a royal charter, recognised by the highest civil authority, the exercise of his ordinary and visitatorial jurisdiction.

The charter of 1264, it must now be noticed, did not create the first body of "Scolares de Merton." It created the first *incorporated* body. It gave a fixity and legal security to a previous disposition of property. It was a development of an earlier idea, and a development that was soon to advance farther, viz., by the strengthening of its academical tie, which was rapidly becoming a cord strong enough to draw the *whole* institution into a local connection with Oxford in addition to the *educational* relation which it had in its most rudimentary state.

With regard to that relation, it is, I fear, impossible at the present day, in our ignorance of the University system on the one hand, and the details of the Merton *ordinatio* on the other, to gain much by speculation.

I entertain no doubt that the phrases, "in scolis degentes," "clericorum in studio degentium," are synonyms, and imply a connection with an University course of study, for the former phrase is continued as the current and formal title of the Fellows after their sole place of residence had become fixed at Oxford; and *studium* is used in the statutes of 1264 as the equivalent of University:— "Oxoniæ, aut alibi, ubi studium viget generale;" which phrase is again varied and explained in the confirmation of 1274 by "Oxoniæ ubi Universitas viget studentium."

The opinion, held by at least one learned man, that *in scolis degere* meant nothing more than the pursuit of a studious life, I cannot reconcile with any of these expressions, and I would appeal farther to an auxiliary clause in the charter of 1262 in favour of *scholæ* meaning a recognised local school of learning:— "Clericorum in scolis degentium, et se *studio* in *eisdem* salubriter applicantium;" and also to the statutes of 1270, which inflict the penalty of "Amotio" on the Fellows, "si præter necessitates domus extra scolas egerint[1]."

I conceive, then, that from the very first the *nepotes* were housed

---

[1] Compare the first Balliol Statutes, 1282 :—"Scolas exerceant et studio intendant secundum Statuta Universitatis Oxoniæ."

chiefly in Oxford in some existing hall, or in some house hired by their uncle, and placed under a licensed Master of Arts for their exclusive use, and that the Warden's main charge was the management of the estate and application of the revenues. This view of his office is the only one given by the assignment:—" Deputati pro conservatione sustentationis prædictæ et rerum et possessionum suarum." A similar one is presented by the statutes, 1264, where the "administratio rerum et possessionum" is the duty specially laid on the Warden; and "Talem studeant nominare qui melior et fidelior in administratione rerum et negotiorum dictæ domus haberi poterit," is the charge given to the electors to the wardenship.

Not until the concentration of the constituent branches of the institution under one domestic government in Oxford were the higher qualifications of the statutes of 1270 required:—"Vir tam in *spiritualibus* quam in temporalibus circumspectus."

And if I am right in the above view of the condition of the original scholars, it will be found to resemble very closely that of other small bodies already existing of " clerici in scolis degentes," whose maintenance was provided for by trusts vested in existing corporations.

Such a trust, we find, was created by Alan Basset, and vested in the priory of Bicester; see A. Wood, Annals, 1243. Such, probably, were some of the earliest provisions for scholars in Cambridge, the exhibitions vested in the priory of Barnwell[k]. Very similar, too, was the trust vested in the University of Oxford by William of Durham's bequest, 1249, for the maintenance of four masters; and very similar likewise was the earliest condition of the Balliol Fellowships, which were merely exhibitions maintaining students *until* the completion of the course of study in Arts under the management of *procuratores,* who represented the founder in the administration of the funds.

And perhaps a still closer similarity existed in the halls supported in Oxford by the religious bodies for the purpose of training their younger members " in scolis Oxoniæ." The best example of this mode of academical provision is to be sought in Gloucester

[k] From a bequest of 200 marks left by Bishop Kilkenny, of Ely. Dugd., *Mon.* The connection of these bequests with masses does not militate against their academical character. All eleemosynary dispositions of the day were framed with a view to secure a return to the donor *in salutem animæ.*

Hall, on the site of which, or not far off, the Benedictine abbey of Winchcombe had a "generale studium" for their novices before 1175, when it is mentioned as part of their property in a papal bull. (Vid. Dugdale's *Mon.*, ii. 854-6.)

In 1258 the present site was purchased by a benefactor for the benefit of Gloucester Abbey, and in 1291, at a general chapter of the Benedictine Order, the hall was adopted as a nursery of students for the whole Order, to be supported by contributions from the richer abbeys.

In this condition it seems to have remained till the Dissolution.

I conceive, then, that the relation of the scholars of Merton to the University before the final concentration of all the members of the body in Oxford, must be gathered from comparisons with those institutions which already existed for the maintenance of "scolares in scolis degentes," to which the founder was in some degree indebted for his model.

But I conceive that he had, at least as early as 1264, the more complete ideal in his mind, and one exclusively of his own conception, viz., that of an incorporated body of secular students, endowed with all the attributes of the great Corporations of Regulars—self-support, self-government, self-replenishment, settled locally in connection with a great seat of study, acquiring a share of that influence in the University which the establishment of powerful monasteries within its bounds had almost monopolized in the hands of the Regulars, and wielding that influence for the benefit of the Church in the advancement of the secular clergy, who, for lack of support and encouragement in the Universities, were sadly decayed in learning.

In the following chapter I must endeavour to examine the documentary matter which exhibits the founder's mind in the further advancement of his institution to its ultimate form, realizing, as I conceive, the complete ideal.

DEED OF ASSIGNMENT REFERRED TO P. 9. (ENDORSED IN LATER HAND.)

" *Carta Walteri de Merton, facta Scolaribus de Merton, et hæc prima de Meandon et de Ffarlee.*

"Omnibus Cristi fidelibus ad quos presens scriptum pervenerit : Walterus de Merton, illustris domini H. regis Angliæ quondam cancellarius, eternam in Domino salutem. Ad omnium vestrum notitiam volo pervenire, quod ego tam auctoritate michi a prefato domino meo rege attributa, necnon potestate michi a capitalibus dominis feodi concessa, quam ratione juris quod michi competit in meis maneriis de Maldon, Chessendone, Farle, assignavi, dimisi, et concessi predicta maneria cum omnibus pertinentiis eorundem, ad sustentationem Johannis de la Clythe, Will. et Rogeri, fratrum ipsius, Roberti fil. Gilberti de Ewell, Philippi fratris sui, Thomæ de Wortynge, Walteri fil. Ricardi Ulvet, Walteri de Portesmue, nepotum meorum, in scholis degentium, secundum ordinationem inde per me factam, necnon a prefato domino rege, et domino I. Wintoniens. episcopo, loci diocesano, et ejus capitulo, approbatam. Ita quoque quod mihi liceat quamcunque voluero scolares alios insimiliter de meis consanguineis vel aliis nominare et assignare qui sustentationem suam inde habeant secundum formam ordinationis prædictæ usque ad numerum in eadem contentum, quam sustentationem prædictis nepotibus meis in scolis degentibus ad totam vitam ipsorum eum pleno Dominio maneriorum predictorum observari volo : nisi aliter et uberius sibi provideatur aut in culpa fuerint quare dicta sustentatione debeant privari ; et similiter aliis meis consanguineis qui ad dictam sustentationem fuerint admissi. Salvis quoad alia omnia conditionibus in supra dicta ordinatione contentis quam etiam ordinationem corrigere mutare et meliorari mihi si expedire videatur pleno jure licebit.

"Salvis etiam michi asiamentis domorum maneriorum ipsorum cum ibi declinare et moram facere voluero, una cum furagio et focalibus et aliis ad sustentationem familiæ meæ necessariis quatenus res ipsa rationabiliter sufficere poterit, prout dictam sustentationem nepotum meorum et aliorum in scolis degentium et ministrorum altaris Christi secundum formam dictæ ordinationis commorantium in maneriis prediotis necnon et custodis dictis scolaribus pro conservatione sustentationis predictæ et rerum ac possessionum suarum deputati seu deinceps deputandi. In hujus autem rei Testimonium præsenti Scripti sigillum meum apponi feci. His testibus Wº. de Brademere, Joh. de Horton, Johē de Arcubus, Philippo le juvene, Hamon de Planat, Brian de Maldon, Will. de Gardiner et aliis."

Seal wholly gone — No date.

CHAPTER III.

THE COMPLETION OF HIS FOUNDATION.

THE main documents to which we must refer as exhibiting the progress of the founder's mind in the perfecting of his institution are the successive statutory documents which he issued or approved, viz. :—

1. A.D. 1264. The earliest extant statutes with royal charter.
2. 1270. The second body of statutes, *tempore pacis*, with royal seal.
3. 1274. Ratification by founder and King Edward I., after final settlement in Oxford.
4. 1276. The ordinations of Archbishop Kilwardby, approved by the founder; and his confirmation, March 13, 1275-6.

The subsidiary documents are the following :—

Deed of assignment, printed p. 9.

1262. License from Richard, Earl of Gloucester.

1264. License from Gilbert, Earl of Gloucester.

1265. Grant from Prior of St. Frideswide of house west of college gate.

1265-6. Epiphany, grant of advowson of St. John's, Oxford.

1266, Aug. 30. Royal charter *de claudendo placeam* [1] *in Oxon.*

—— Sept. 7. Royal charter giving advowson of St. Peter's for impropriation.

1266. Sale by Jacob, son of Mosey the Jew, of London, of house near college gate.

1267, Sept. 3. Royal charter for bringing water from the Cherwell "ad locum scolarium Oxon," transcribed by Kilner.

1275. Confirmation by Archbishop Peckham and provincial synod at Reading.

1276. Confirmation by Gravesend, Bishop of Lincoln.

1280. Confirmation by Pope Nic. III.

1284. Archbishop Peckham's injunctions, entitled *Interpretatio Statutorum.*

---

[1] The space, then void, between St. John's Church and the city wall, now called Merton Grove. A right to go to the wall *tempore guerræ* was reserved to the townsmen.

1340. The statutes of Peterhouse, Cambridge, remodelled by Bishop Montague of Ely, "secundam regulam Mertonensem."

It is readily seen from these documents that there was a steady progress during the decad 1264-74, towards—

1. The concentration of the institution in Oxford.
2. The full development of its literary and religious objects.

The statutes of 1264 exhibit to us an institution divided in locality, the head with the œconomical and ecclesiastical part of the body living in one place, in the country; the academical in another, where its academical functions could be effectively pursued. That this academical place was Oxford I feel no doubt, though the statutes do not tie the scholars to the Oxford schools, but only give it the preference implied by its being the only place of study specified "in scholis degentium Oxon aut alibi ubi studium vigere contigerit."

The academical portion consisted of twenty scholars, the ecclesiastical of two or three *ministri altaris*, the œconomical of the serving and farming brethren, who seem to be covered by the general name of *fratres*, which occurs in all the early designations of the college, even when "minister" is omitted.

I have stated my reasons for thinking that the scholars were occupying a hall in Oxford previously to 1264. I assume this to be certain from the period of the first charter in that year. Very soon after, we find the founder acquiring property in the city, and on the present site of the college. In 1265 he obtains a grant from the prior of St. Frideswide of the house standing to the westward of the present gateway. In the very beginning of 1265-6 he obtained the rectory of St. John Baptist, which gave him command of the ground and some houses immediately adjoining the church. In the ensuing August he obtained the king's license *de claudendo placeam*, which gave him command over the whole space between the church and the city walls.

On September 7 he got the king's grant of a far more important boon,—important enough of itself to have decided him in attaching his college to Oxford,—the gift of the advowson and rectory of St. Peter's-in-the-East, with a view to its impropriation. This gift, when completed by the act of impropriation following the death of the last rector, Bogo de St. Clare, the king's uncle, in 1294, placed the college in possession of the whole parish of Holywell, and of the tithes of Wolvercot. In this year, too, he bought of Jacob, son of Mosey, a London Jew, another house, fronting the street of St. John Bapt.

Had the founder not already succeeded in acquiring an ample footing by this time within the walls, I conclude he would have turned his attention to the Holywell manor as the more desirable site.

But we can have little doubt but that in 1267 he was possessor of a tract reaching from the church of St. John up to the city wall on the east, and bounded by the same on the south; of the greater part, in short, of what forms the College gardens[m]: for on Sept. 3 he acquired from his royal patron a privilege which implies a most fixed purpose as to the ultimate location of his scholars.

This privilege is conveyed by a license empowering him to cut a canal from some point in the Cherwell above Holywell Church through the precincts of St. John's Hospital, now Magdalen College, and passing outside the East-gate, near the barton[n] of St. Frideswide, to enter through the city wall, and so through the present garden by the college, "ad emundationes curiæ suæ," with outlet through the city wall near the 'domus' of St. Frideswide.

The settlement of the academical branch of this institution must then be considered as completed by this date; the concentration of the branches still tarried.

In 1270 the founder issued his statutes afresh for the purpose of ratifying in time of peace the disposition of his estates which he had made "tempore turbationis Angliæ," and for the sake of adding newly acquired property and increasing the numbers of his scholars, but he does not mention any change of locality.

This was reserved till 1274, when he obtained a charter from the young king ratifying all his gifts of land, with the latest additions, and his previous *regula*, or statutes, and transferring the seat of his domus from Malden to the site in Oxford, "ubi perpetuo scholares meos moraturos esse decerno."

In 1274, then, Oxford beheld the first *perfected* corporation of secular scholars established within her academical and municipal precincts, provided with all needful powers and ratifications from

---

[m] Completed by a further grant from Edward II., March 20, 1309.

[n] This barton, or grange, is still standing at the entrance of Christ Church meadow from Rose-lane.

the authorities of Church and State, and destined to enter upon a course of great literary and religious benefit,—a course to be prolonged far beyond the life of its then eminent rivals, the established houses of Regulars in Oxford, and destined, too, to be the parent of a succession of similar institutions. ·

The question what was the exact position which the founder designed the institution to fill is a very interesting one. It will be best answered by looking at the state of the University, of the Church, and of learning in his time, and will perhaps never be perfectly answered until the condition of the times is more fully brought to light.

In the first half of the thirteenth century, in spite of the unsettledness of the times, the weakness of the government, and the corruptions of the Church, the Oxford schools were producing great men, and exercising a large influence both in the Church and the world of letters [o].

The first efforts of the new order of friars were directed to the two ancient Universities as important seats of influence. The Dominicans and Franciscans both established themselves in Oxford and Cambridge in 1221, very soon after their introduction into England, and opened schools which were taught by most able readers, and became great centres of attraction.

The lately published letters of Adam de Marisco, who was one of the ablest of the early readers in Oxford [p], exhibit a most instructive view of the vast amount of influence, ecclesiastical and political, which followed from the academical success of the friars. In one (No. 242) we find him introducing "honorabilem virum Walterum de Merton," then about to seek subdeacon's orders at the hands of Bishop Grostete, to a brother friar who was probably about the bishop's person.

One glance at the accompanying table, shewing the Oxford institutions of that century, will prove how zealously the religious orders struggled to plant themselves in the University, and what vast vantage-ground they had secured by their activity :—

INSTITUTIONS OF OXFORD—THIRTEENTH CENTURY.

Founded.
727. Priory of St. Frideswide, ultimately Benedictine.
1129. Abbey of Oseney, Augustinian Canons; founded by Robert

---

[o] See A. Wood's Annals under the years 1221, 1227 and 1228.
[p] In the *Monumenta Franciscana*, edited by Rev. J. S. Brewer.

D'Oily, and including, in 1149, his uncle's foundation of Canons of the Church of St. George-in-the-Castle.

1221. Franciscans, established in St. Ebbe's.

Dominicans, established in the Jewry, St. Edward's Parish, removed forty years later to the island near Littlegate, now called the Friars.

1233. St. John's Hospital, refounded by Henry III. on site of Magdalen College.

1252. Augustinian Friars, or Eremites, on site of Wadham College. Confirmed by Henry III. and Bogo the Rector of St. Peter's, 1268-9. Mentioned in University statute, *circa* 1267, as taking part in disputations.

1254. (Within ten years of arrival in England), Carmelite, or White Friars, in parish of St. George-in-the-Castle: transferred to Beaumont Palace 1313, by Edward II.

1262. (Five years after arrival), Friars de Pœnitentia, or de Sacco; without the West-gate, till suppression of the order in 1309, when the site was given to the Franciscans. They addicted themselves to learning like the other orders.

1271. Gloucester Hall, adopted by a general chapter of the Benedictine order as a seminary for younger members. A house on or near this site had belonged to Winchcombe Abbey as early as 1149. Vid. Dug. Mon., Abb. Winch.

1281. Cistercian Abbey of Rewley, refounded by Edmund, Earl of Cornwall. Created by his father Richard King of the Romans some years earlier. Called in the Cistercian Annals " Studium Oxoniæ."

1290. Durham College, founded by the Prior of Durham as a seminary for novices: enlarged 1333, by Bishop Bury of Durham.

1291. The Brethren of the Holy Trinity, established by Edmund, Earl of Cornwall, at the East-gate, for the sake of academical benefits to their novices. See A. Wood's "Annals."

Add to these:—

1249. The bequest[q] to the University by William of Durham for

---

[q] In the year 1249 Matthew of Paris records that the Cistercians obtained the privilege "exercere scolas Universitatum." The ground for seeking it was "ne forent contemptui prædicatoribus, minoribus, et sæcularibus litteratis, præcipue legistis et decretalibus." He adds that they provided themselves noble abodes at Paris and

the maintenance of four poor Masters of Arts, out of which bequest University College has grown.

1282. The endowment of poor scholars and first settlement under statutes by Dervorguilla de Balliol.

The Crossed, or Crutched Friars, who were removed to the neighbourhood of the East-gate, in St. Peter's parish, were first settled near South-gate, probably in this century. They were a very small foundation, perhaps of no scholastic importance.

Bishop Kennett, in his "Parochial Antiquities," p. 214, bears his testimony to the fact that the Religious had by custom schools in Oxford for the benefit of their houses, which schools commonly bore the name of their owners. He mentions particularly Dorchester, Eynsham, St. Frideswide, Littlemore, Oseney, Studley. Two schools, called St. Patrick's, were given to St. Frideswide's Priory by Master John, son of Hamo, a mercer, about 1255, and the Civil Law School in St. Edward's parish also belonged to the Priory. See Dugd. Mon., Priory of St. Frid.

In Cambridge, we learn from Dean Peacock, in his Appendix to Observations to University Statutes, 1841, that the four chief orders of Friars, Carmelites, Franciscans, Dominicans, Augustinians, were all established in the thirteenth century, and wielded a powerful influence within the University.

The statutes continually deal with them, assign them their place in University processions, limit the number of their incepting graduates, and betray the same jealousy of their activity and influence as the statutes of Paris and of Oxford.

Besides the Friars, the Priory of Barnwell and other smaller religious houses, now merged in St. John's and other colleges, exercised large influence in University matters.

Our founder's purpose I conceive to have been to secure for his own order in the Church, for the secular priesthood, the academical benefits which the religious orders were so largely enjoying, and to this end I think all his provisions are found to be consistently framed.

---

elsewhere, "ubi scolæ viguerunt;" and further, that cloister religion was much out of vogue, and St. Benedict's rule of forsaking the study of literature well-nigh forgotten. He might have added that the more recent and more stringent rules of St. Francis and St. Dominic to the same effect were equally forgotten by their early followers.

He borrowed from the monastic institutions the idea of an aggregate body living by common rule, under a common head, provided with all things needful for a corporate and perpetual life, fed by its secured endowments, fenced from all external interference, except that of its lawful patron; but after borrowing thus much, he differenced his institution by giving his beneficiaries quite a distinct employment, and keeping them free from all those perpetual obligations which constituted the essence of the religious life.

His beneficiaries are from the first designated as "scolares in scolis degentes," their employment was study, not what was technically called the religious life, either the "claustralis religio" of the older orders, as Matt. Paris calls it (A.D. 1249,) or the newly introduced "religio" of St. Francis and St. Dominic. He forbad his scholars ever to take vows, they were to keep themselves free of every other institution, to enter no one else's *obsequium.* He looked forward to their going forth to labour *in sæculo*, and acquiring preferment and property, "si quis in uberrimam fortunam devenerit." Study being the function of the inmates of his house, their time was not to be taken up by ritual or ceremonial duties, for which special chaplains were appointed; neither was it to be bestowed on any handicrafts, as in some monastic orders. Voluntary poverty was not enjoined, though poor circumstances were a qualification for a fellowship. No austerity was required, though contentment with simple fare was enforced as a duty, and the system of enlarging the number of inmates according to the means of the house was framed to keep the allowance to each at the very moderate rate which the founder fixed.

The proofs of the founder's design to benefit the Church through a better-educated secular priesthood, are to be found, not in the letter of the statutes, but in the tenor of their provisions, especially as to studies, in the direct averments of some of the subsidiary documents, in the fact of his providing Church patronage as part of his system, and in the readiness of prelates and chapters to grant him impropriations of the rectorial endowments of the Church.

The statutes, like many a document set forth by a man thoroughly possessed with a leading idea, never expressly set forth that idea. "In honorem Divini nominis," "in profectum ecclesiæ," "pro utilitate ecclesiastici regiminis," are the wide phrases of the statutes conveying his general purpose, which is much more closely described by his patrons in their grants and confirmations.

Thus his feudal lord in 1262 describes the object of the Malden House as "ad sustentationem clericorum in scolis degentium et in studio salubriter in iis applicantium, quos in domo Domini veluti columnas, et fulcimenta speramus Domino largiter profecturos."

In 1275-6 Archbishop Kilwardby grants his confirmation to the completed foundation, describing its object as that of producing by education in arts, canon law, and theology, a "copia doctorum qui velut stellæ in perpetuas eternitates mansuri valeant ad justitiam plurimos erudire."

The bishops at the synod of Reading, 1279, grant their confirmation in terms equally significant, and Pope Nicolas III. in 1280, in his Bull of ratification, expresses his value for the institution: "Quod per viros litterarum scientia redimitos fides Catholica robur suscipit et ecclesia multipliciter decoratur."

We may add to this a series of testimonials, lay and clerical, to the fact that the college did bear good fruit to the Church, in the very way intended; for early in the reign of Edward III., when the college was moving the court of Rome for the impropriation of the rectory of Emildon, it armed itself with recommendations from the king, archbishop, and bishop of Durham. The king designates the college as a "Promptuarium ad dandam scientiam Salutis plebi ejus a quo educti sunt hactenus viri perfecti, quorum doctrinâ longè latèque Ecclesiam pervenit spiritalis gratia multiformis." See Rymer's *Fœd.*, tom. iv. 1330.

Bishop Beaumont, 1330, testifies "quod totam Ecclesiam Anglicanam fructuosis operibus et doctrinis perlustravit."

After another century's experience, we find a still stronger testimonial to its having borne the fruit intended, and that from a monarch who was a watchful observer of educational institutions, and had just then appointed a member of the Merton family both by kin and by education, Henry Sever, as the provost of his new college of Eton. In a writ (penes Coll. Mert.) of the 22nd of his reign, 1444, bearing the authority of Parliament, and enrolled in the Exchequer, he exempts the college property from taxation on the ground of its great services: "Quod plurimæ columpnæ sacrosanctæ Ecclesiæ fuerunt educatæ omni generi scientiarum ac virtutum fulgentes et totum Christianismum per eorum scripta illustrantes.... Nos volentes inopiæ tam celebris collegii, quod regnum nostrum, immo totam Ecclesiam in ejus alumpnis ita insigniter decoravit, in aliquo subvenire, ne (quod absit) Coll. illud, cujus sancta statuta, ceremoniæ, ac religiosus sociorum convictus, in aliis regni nostri utriusque Universitatis Collegiis mutativè, velud imago parentis in Prole relucent." There are many other passages as strongly declaring the founder's intention to make his institution serviceable " ad profectum Ecclesiæ," which shew both that its literary functions were subservient to that object, and that the charitable consideration, both towards his own kindred and towards the poor and unaided scholar, though ever present to his mind, were all subordinated to the main end of benefiting the Church by erecting a nursery for her parochial priesthood in the bosom of the University.

An inspection of the founder's provisions and regulations will lead us to see how consistently and wisely he framed his means to his purposed end.

And first, in looking at his prescribed course of study, we find that it is all pointed to the perfecting of the theologian, who was in due course to go forth and labour in one of the benefices attached to the house, or in whatever field might be opened to him.

But the course did not begin with theology, for a very good reason. One of the great causes of weakness which then affected theological study, was the neglect of the needful foundation which the University intended to provide in her course of arts. Antony Wood, in his Annals of this century, dwells much upon this evil. He asserts that the Bishops admitted mere boys of twenty to holy orders, who consequently hurried rapidly onwards to the attainment of that small degree of theological learning which could be expected at such an age. He preserves some ludicrous instances of the ignorance of grammar.

Another cause which weakened theology, was greediness of the more profitable study of canon and civil law.

To remedy these weaknesses, the founder introduced his *Grammaticus*[r] as officer of his institution. He required the *pars major*

---

[r] " Sit etiam grammaticus unus, qui studio grammaticæ totaliter vacet, sibique, de bonis domus, librorum copia et alia necessaria ministrentur, et eorum qui studio grammaticæ [in hujusmodi rudimentis, stat. 1270], fuerint applicati, curam habeat;. et ad ipsum etiam provectiores in dubiis suæ facultatis habeant absque rubore regres-

of the *scolares,* "ut artium liberalium et studio philosophiæ vacent," but this only as introductory to, and qualifying for, their final study of theology, "donec in his laudabiliter provecti ad studium se transferant theologiæ." His regulation touching the study of the laws, is restrictive as to the number privileged to proceed, and their qualification. "Quatuor* autem vel quinque, ex sui superioris providentia, quos ipse humiles et ad hoc aptos decreverit, in jure canonico licenter studeant."—[Stat. 1274, cap. ii.] And for their improvement in this faculty, the Warden was to allow them at times "ut jura civilia audiant."

The prescribed course of study then, was as follows:—

1. Grammar, under the *Grammaticus,* for those who needed, ["rudimenta puerilia," stat. 1270.]

2. Arts and philosophy, in accordance with the University course of the day, for *all.*

3. Theology, for *all, after* proficiency in arts.

4. Canon law, for four or five select proficients in theology, and *pro utilitate ecclesiastici regiminis,* with so much of civil as might be ancillary to canon law.

Here, then, we see the provision made by a wise and pious man, desiring to remedy the injury which sound learning and true religion had suffered, on the one hand from the neglect of elementary knowledge, and on the other from greedy pursuit of the honours and profits of the laws.

Whilst he provides for a good liberal education, and general grounding in all subsidiary knowledge, he jealously guards his main object of theological study both from being attempted too early by the half-educated boy, and from being abandoned too soon for the temptations of something more profitable. It should be remarked

---

sum. Sub cujus magisterio scolares ipsi . . . . latino fruantur eloquio ceu idiomate vulgari." Stat. 1274, cap. ii.

Degrees in grammar were anciently conferred by all Universities, until the improvement of classical knowledge arising from the art of printing. The Elizabethan Statutes, second code, extinguished the degree in the University of Cambridge; but only fifty years earlier Bishop Stanley of Ely had founded a grammar-præceptorship at Jesus College. See Dean Peacock's note, p. xxx., in his Appendix to Cambridge Stat.

* A very small proportion of the number to which the founder expected his scholars to grow; see his provision for deans over *twenties,* cap. vii. The study of law is clearly viewed as a privilege, and a reward of moral and other qualities. In Stat. 1270, was added, "pro utilitate ecclesiastici regiminis, secundum quod modesti, humiles, honesti extiterint, et eos Custos zelum Dei et animarum habere noverit."

E

that whilst the Warden is charged with the duty of keeping an illiterate youth from commencing the crowning study, he has no authority for dispensing with it in any one case. He was required to dismiss the idle member who neglected to qualify himself by steady progress in the lower branches[t].

It will be seen here how the founder was working in unison with the sounder part of the University, for in 1251 that body found it expedient to enact some restraints upon the hasty acquirement of the higher divinity degrees. It was in the same spirit, and to remedy the same evil, that Walter de Merton forbad his members to enter the faculty at all before a full proficiency in arts and philosophy, acquired both *audiendo* and *regendo*, i. e. both by attending the schools as undergraduate listeners, and by teaching in the schools as *magistri artium*.

That his restraints were aimed at no imaginary evils will be proved by reference to two facts, the one occurring in Archbishop Pekham's ordinances, 1284, the other in some capitular orders made by the college in 1455.

Archbishop Pekham we find rebuking some of the Fellows for proceeding to the profitable study of medicine, under pretence that it fell within the prescript study of philosophy[u], and others for a grosser violation of statute by proceeding to an unlicensed study of the laws[x].

The orders of 1455 proceed upon the fact that great disgrace had accrued to the college from the rejection of Fellows at the Bishop's examination, and impose an oath to the effect that no one would proceed to holy orders before the completed term of Regency in Arts.

We may here remark that having been so explicit in the prescription of studies, the founder did not deem it needful to legislate for the professions which his Fellows were to pursue. Were a Brunel or a Stephenson in this nineteenth century founding a college for

---

[t] "Si studere neglexerit" is a "causa amotionis;" and also "diutina ægritudo," making a Fellow "ad studium inutilis."—Stat. 1274, capp. iv., xiv.

[u] Medicine nevertheless afterwards became a flourishing study in the college during the fourteenth, fifteenth, and sixteenth centuries, and in a capitular order of 1504 is recognised as a "philosophical art."

[x] His interpretation of the statutable meaning of "philosophy," and his reference to the practice in the founder's time, are very useful as comments on the statutable course of study.

the improvement of his own order of civil engineers, after framing a course of study directed throughout to the perfecting of the student in the practice of an engineer's calling, he might well omit, either consciously or unconsciously, all regulation as to his ultimate profession. In the parallel case, viz. the secular priest of the thirteenth century erecting an institution for the improvement of his own order, there were reasons why it was less needful for him to lay down any regulations as to the ultimate destination of students whose whole antecedents he so modelled from the most elementary stage of their education, as to make it their interest, as well as their duty, to enter the sacred profession. There is no doubt that the prescribed course of theology was intended to carry them to the higher degrees in that faculty, which, after the University requirement of a Latin sermon in 1251, could only be obtained by an ordained candidate. Beyond this, again, lay the prospect of a college benefice, furnishing another inducement to enter the priesthood, to say nothing of the universal usage of the day, perhaps as influential as any other cause, according to which, admission into the clerical body was deemed a qualification for the pursuit of every learned profession.

The fact, then, of the founder's omitting to designate the future profession of the boys whom he admitted to his institution need cause no doubt whatever as to his intentions.

We may proceed now to notice another provision, which indicates the close connection between the foundation and the secular priesthood, his large provision of Church-patronage.

That patronage should have been bestowed upon him for the benefit of his institution, in whatever way it was to benefit the Church, was not surprising, when we consider that the highest personages of the realm were deeply interested in the ex-Chancellor's undertaking, and that the bestowal of advowsons was, to great feudal chiefs, the easiest mode of befriending Church institutions, and a most effective one where it was followed (as was commonly the case in the thirteenth century) by impropriation of the rectory; but it is plain that he bestirred himself to obtain the patronage of preferments, for which he had no doubt to pay some adequate price to the former patrons. The right of advowson seems, therefore, to have been of itself an object, and the nomination of his scholars to benefices, where they might bestow the fruits of their academical

urse in the midst of an illiterate clergy and a rude half-barbarous
ity, appears to have made an integral portion of his scheme. Of
s royal patrons every one bestowed an advowson upon him. The
ng gave the rectory of St. Peter's-in-the-East, Oxford, with its
lapels of Holywell and Wolvercot; Richard, his brother, gave
orspath; the king's sons, Edward and Edmund, gave Elham in
ent, and Emildon in Northumberland[y].

These, we may suppose, were gratuitous gifts, but we cannot
ppose that the conventual bodies, which granted five of the re-
aining advowsons, so freely alienated their corporate property.
he abbeys of Reading and Tyrone (France), the priories of Stone
Staffordshire), Merton, Tortington (Sussex), granted respectively
e advowsons of St. John's, Oxon, Stratton, Wilts., Wolford with
urmington, Malden, and Farleigh, and certainly to three of these
anters some return was made[z]. Gamlingay (one moiety), Lap-
orth, Ponteland, Cuxham, and Ibstone, were besides acquired
om lay patrons, and probably were duly paid for. When we
nsider that the right of patronage thus bestowed upon the col-
ge enabled it to nominate no less than seventeen of its members
endowed cures, it is impossible to resist the belief that the ac-
usition of this patronage was not the result of chance circum-
ances or of the donor's convenience, but an integral part of the
under's scheme, carrying on his scholars beyond the term of their
ademic life, and bestowing their spiritual things on the very
aces from which they should derive their temporal sustenance.

Another proof of the founder's mind is seen in the fact of his dis-
untenancing the lucrative professions which were then open to
e clergy, and which were likely to tempt the more able of his
holars to abandon the steady pursuit of their sacred calling. We
ave already seen how jealously he restrained his advancing student
om running off from the more barren study of theology, how he

---

[y] All these were given with license of impropriation, and all (except Horspath, of
hich, for some reason, the college never got possession) were impropriated, and, with
e other impropriate rectories, Ponteland, Wolford, Stratton, and Gamlingay, form a
eat proportion of the present college property.

[z] To the abbey of Reading a quit-rent was paid long after the foundation. The
bey of Tyrone was recompensed by the purchase of a quit-rent for the benefit of its
ll at Andewell, Hants. See Stratton Evidences, (penes Coll. Mert.)

The prior of Tortington owns that the founder had *contented* him, " Ex curialitate
ia, quamquam ad hoc minime teneretur." See Farleigh Evidences, (penes Coll. Mert.)

confined the study of canon law with its more gainful prospects to a privileged few, advanced theologians, and that "pro utilitate ecclesiastici regiminis," and how he permitted the study of civil law only as ancillary to the canon, but we have a clearer enunciation of his mind in the Injunctions (already adverted to) of his almost-cotemporary, Abp. Pekham, when in 1284 he felt it his duty to the founder to banish all study of medicine from the college, and to restrain the canonists to the licensed number. He declares, on his own knowledge, that in the founder's time no *medici* had been allowed in the college, and that on the principle of "consuetudo est juris interpres," he must, as acting for the founder, exclude them utterly.

We do not conceive, then, that there need remain any doubt that the particular benefit which the founder designed to confer on the Church was the improvement of his own order, the secular priesthood, by giving them first a good elementary, and then a good theological, education, in close union with a University, and with the moral and religious training of a scholar-family living under rules of piety and discipline. And this design was, we have good reason to believe, in the main achieved. Whilst the Visitor of 1284 brings to light the fact that worldliness and selfishness were in some degree marring the original design, there are abundant witnesses to its general success. During the first eighty years of the life of the institution, a brilliant succession of names, divines who were also scholars and philosophers, shone forth, and kindled other founders to devote their substance to the creation of similar nurseries of learned clergy. The earlier statutes of Balliol, University, Oriel, Peterhouse (Cambridge), all borrowed, with more or less of closeness and avowal, the *Regula Mertonensis*, and thus justified the assertion which the royal founder of Eton afterwards used, that the later colleges bore a childlike resemblance to their common parent, "velut imago parentis in prole, relucent."

CHAPTER IV.

FROM THE FOUNDATION OF HIS COLLEGE TO HIS DEATH.

AT the close of chapter I. our attention was called off from following the thread of the founder's life to the consideration of the greatest surviving achievement of his life, the foundation of his college.

We must now resume that thread from 1264, and state such few facts as are known of his history during the remaining thirteen years of his vigorous and useful career. In doing this, we must stand excused if we recapitulate a few facts which have been already mentioned in connection with the foundation of the college.

In 1265-6 we find him busy in acquiring property in Oxford. He purchased in 1265 two tenements* situate east of the church of St. John, (vid. supra, p. 17,) and also obtained a grant from the abbey of Reading of a mansion west of that church, to which the right of the patronage [b] appertained.

The deed of purchase of the second house brings to light a curious fact. The owner, Jacob, son of Master Mosey the Jew, of London, had let the house for the residence of Thomas and Antony Bek, sons of the Baron of Grimsthorpe, Lincolnshire, who must have been boys following their academical studies. The seller therefore remits part of the price, in consideration of his tenants being allowed to remain for the next three years from Michaelmas. It seems probable that the founder took them under his charge, and received them as, what have since been called, fellow-commoners, for he became attached to the younger Antony, who was afterwards (1280) known as the Fighting Bishop of Durham, and titular Patriarch of Jerusalem, and he bequeathed to him his best gold ring.

---

[a] After acquiring the house of Flixthorpe in 1268, he probably had possession of nearly all the present street-frontage of the college.

[b] Confirmed by the king in 1266, and appropriated to the college, together with the rectory of St. Peter's, by Gravesend, Bishop of Lincoln, and his chapter, in Sept. 1266. The writ of induction to St. Peter's was granted by Bishop Sutton in 1294, upon the death of the last spiritual rector, Bogo de St. Clare; transcribed by Kilner, App. vi. The college obtained induction to St. John's in 1292.

On Oct. 5, 1265, the king granted to the founder, by the title of Canon of St. Paul's, a marsh or fen called la More [c], reputed anciently to have belonged to his prebend of Holywell, or Finsbury, forfeited to the crown by the City of London on account of their conduct in the late troubles, when they sacked the Canon's house.

On Oct. 6, 1265, the king again made use of his ascendancy, established by the battle of Evesham Aug. 4, to add another favour to his former ones. He granted the founder the forfeited estate of Robert Fitz-neale (*filius Nigelli*), who had joined in Montfort's rebellion, provided it did not exceed £100 per annum. This man had married one of the founder's nieces. A reference to the uncle's will, as given in the Appendix, will shew that a truly loving spirit had prompted him to use his influence with the Crown for the rescue of the estate, which, by bequest, he restored to its former owner. Vide notes on Will, App., p. iii. Kilner transcribes the grant; see MS., App. viii.

In October, 1266, the convent of Stone, in Staffordshire, granted the advowson of Wolford, with Burmington chapel, in Warwickshire. The fine passed in consequence of this grant dates in the ensuing Hilary Term, Jan. 27, 1266-7, (vid. Dugdale's "Warwickshire").

In September, 1267, the royal license (vid. supra, p. 15) to cut a canal from the Cherwell was issued. Whether this power was acted upon immediately or not, there is no certain record. The names of three Fellows, John de Abingdon, William Harrington, and Symon Yefley (Iffley), are mentioned as the committee appointed by the college to execute the work, and they are known to belong to the reign of Edward II. Probably so large and costly a work was long in hand, if ever it reached completion [d]. Dr. Astrey in his MS. life

---

[c] Magna Mora was the name of that region which is now teeming with population under the names of Finsbury, Moorfields, Moorgate, but was then qualified to afford a fishery to the citizens. See Stow's Survey of London, by Strype, vol. ii. b. iv. p. 53. The citizens refused seisin of the moor in spite of the king's grant, and in 1271 it was needful to summon Walter Hervey, the mayor. The Canon appears to have got his seisin, for his successor, fifty years after, ceded the debateable ground to the City for xx*. per annum. Vide *Lib. de Antiquis Leg. penes Civ. Lond.*, fol. 141. b; and *Registr. Capit. S. Pauli Pyx. T.*

[d] If completed, I conceive that the cut began at what is now called Parson's Pleasure; that it passed in a straight line, as now seen, to Holywell-mill, and to the western end of Magdalen-bridge, serving the hospital of St. John "in emundationem curiæ suæ," as it does now; then it must have turned towards the north-east corner

of the founder affirms that the water was brought to the college in force sufficient to drive a mill, and rests for his proof on Thomas Hearne, (*MSS. Collectanea,* vol. lxxxviii. pp. 24, 33). With regard to the mill, there are certainly entries in bursars' rolls of the fourteenth century recording repairs of a mill, but as horse-mills were so common in those ages, we cannot venture to affirm that these entries prove the existence of a water-mill turned by the far-fetched water of the Cherwell.

We must not pass on without noticing the fact that there is a copy of statutes in the Merton Exchequer, (referred to by Ant. Wood, Hist. Oxon, lib. i. pp. 29, 33, as being in Pyx Oxon. A, 1, 2,) which bears the date Jan. 1267. This document strangely gainsays its own date by declaring the decease of Hen. III., which took place in 1272, and by bearing the founder's episcopal seal, which did not exist till 1274. It has misled all writers till Kilner, who has shewn that the date is in error, and supposes the document to be an exemplar or confirmation by the founder, *after* his consecration, of his last and final settlement of his college issued in August, 1274. Kilner gives instances of similar errors or dates in Merton documents[e].

The year 1263 witnessed further accessions to the college property. The first was the gift by Prince Edward[f], the heir of the throne, of the advowson of Elham in Kent, followed by the impropriation[g] of it by Archbishop Boniface, "in perpetuos et proprius usus domus scholarium de Merton apud Meandon fundatæ."

The second was the impropriation[h] by Giffard, Bp. of Worcester, of the rectory of Wolford, given in 1266 by the priory of Stone.

The king's favour, too, was again shewn by a grant, addressed to

---

of Merton gardens, and passed through the city wall, where there is still an underground arch, and so to the college. The level of the great quadrangle has been raised artificially eight or ten feet, and probably most of the garden has gained in height.

[e] Vide note in Astrey's MS. Life of Founder, p. 24.

[f] The Prince's arms appear in the east window of the chapel, with those of the king and the Earl of Gloucester, in acknowledgment of him as one of three most signal patrons.

[g] April 20, confirmed by chapter of Canterbury May 26. *Reg. Eccl. Christi Cant.* The Archbishop retained the right of nominating the person to be presented by the college for institution.

[h] "Salvâ portione vicarii," which portion was settled Sept. 24, 1270, by episcopal "ordinatio," at £10 per annum. Reg. Giffard, fol. 7. The rectory and vicarage were again united June 17, 1279, and another appropriation was obtained from Bishop Cobham July 20, 1322.

the constables of the Tower of London and of Windsor Castle, of free water-carriage for a year by the river Thames, for all the grain, wood, or hày[l] of Walter de Merton[k], "dilectus familiaris noster."

It appears also from the Patent Rolls of the following year, (53 Henry III., m. 19,) that he was permitted by the king to compound for the tenth granted by the pope[l] to the king of all ecclesiastical revenues for three years. The collector of the tenth reports that he had received nothing from the church of Linton, diocese of Bath and Wells, because the rector, Walter de Merton, had compounded . with the king for one mark[m].

This document exhibits the founder not only as a canon of Wells[n], but as having presented himself to the church of Litton[o] in his canon's right.

The founder again appears in 1268-9, as a counsellor to the Crown, though in no recognised office. In the Patent Rolls, 53 Henry III., m. 25, No. 1, *a tergo*, (entered also in the Red Book of the Exchequer,) there is an ordinance in Norman-French, bearing this title, "Provisiones de Judaismo liberatæ ad Scaccarium per Dom. Walt. de Merton."

The nature of these provisions and of the events which led to them are fully related by a dutiful son of Merton, Dr. Tovey, in his *Anglia Judaica*, who also adds *verbatim* the writ to the Barons of the Exchequer for executing the provisions. His whole chapter is one of interest to the Oxford and especially to the Merton reader, for it relates, as the cause which altered the king's policy towards his Jewish subjects, and probably animated Walter de Merton's provisions, the daring outrage of an Oxford Jew upon the most sacred symbol of Christianity, upon the cross itself, whilst borne in procession by the monks of St. Frideswide in the neighbourhood of their church, on Ascension-day, 1268. Prince Edward, who was in the town at the time, seems to have stirred up his less vigorous father to a determined chastisement of the offence. The king

---

[l] Patent, 52 Henry VIII., m. 21.

[k] This freed him from the toll called "Avalagium," which Rapin mentions vol. i. p. 214.

[l] The Bull dates Viterbo, June 9, 1267. See Charters, 51 Henry III., m. 10.

[m] Kilner found evidence of this payment in the return from the King's Commissioners, "ad audiend. compot. de variis Ecclesiis," &c.

[n] Vid. note in Dr. Astrey's MS. Hist. of Founder, p. 24.

[o] Linton, now called Litton, is a small parish on Mendip, in the gift of the prebendary of Litton.

F

required the Oxford Jews, who would not surrender the offender, to build a marble cross near the scene of the offence, " in placca scolarium de Merton^p," and to deposit a cross of silver in the college for use at future public processions.

We can hardly doubt that the founder's counsel was prompting the king in this determined policy, which he had to push yet farther on account of the dogged resistance and trickery of the offenders^q.

On Dec. 20, 1269, another instance occurs of the founder's continued influence with the king, and presence about his person. The king^r then renewed a very important grant to the canons of Sarum of tithes of his forests, in Wilts., Dorset, and Berks., " ad instantiam dilecti et familiaris nostri Walteri de Merton."

Probably in this year he purchased the estate at Cambridge *cum membris* of the Dunnings, who had held it from the Conquest, and lately mortgaged it to Guy of Castle Bernard and Will. de Manefend his nephew. The capital messuage of this property is the old Norman mansion of the Dunnings, near the castle, still existing, with its crypt of sixty feet long and other Norman features.

The year 1270 stands as a notable one in Merton history, as giving birth to the second body of statutes, issued for the purpose of confirming, " tempore pacis," the disposition of his estates which the founder had made " tempore turbationis Angliæ," i.e. 1264, and of adding thereto his later acquisitions.

By the charter which contains the statutes, and is ratified by royal authority, he settles upon his college the additional manors of Stillington, Kibworth, Cuxham^s, Ibstone, Chetingdon and Thorncroft, Gamlingay-Merton, Over-Merton, and Chesterton, in Cambridgeshire, lands at Seaton, and houses in Cambridge, the

---

^p See Tovey for the writs *in extenso.* The cross was seen by John Ross, who studied at Oxford *temp.* Hen. VI., somewhat decayed, but still exhibiting its inscription. It stood to the westward of the church, at the north entrance of Merton Grove. The silver cross was afterwards given to the charge of St. Frideswide's Priory.

^q In 1290 the Jews were banished, to the number of 15,000 or 16,000, and did not return to the realm till the Rebellion.

^r At Clarendon, near Sarum. See Pat. 54 Hen. VII., m. 25.

^s This manor he charges with an annuity of £20 per annum to his hospital at Basingstoke, till it should be provided with an equivalent. Other estates, e.g. Kibworth and Malden, he charged with pensions to his kindred, and with the liability of entertaining him and his retinue on occasions, at a fixed rate for fuel and horse-provender.

advowsons of Ponteland, Dodington, Horspath, Wolford, Lapworth, Stratton, Elham, and St. Peter's-in-the-East.

This charter makes no difference in the constitution of the college. It is still the "Domus apud Meandon" (Maldon), with its "scolares in scolis apud Oxon vel alibi studentium;" but there is an indication of the coming change, in the provision that the translation of the college should not void any legal rights of property, as long as there was no union with any other college. A provision, too, occurs for the annual re-union of the divided portions of the body, requiring that eight or ten of the seniors should yearly, on the feast of St. Kenelm (July 17), repair to the house at Maldon, "in signum proprietatis et dominii," and then inquire into the Warden's administration of the estates, with leave to extend their stay to eight or ten days.

A note at the end of this charter ought not to go unnoticed. "Mem. quod de manerio de Kibworth sustentari debent pro anima Henrici de Aleman (Henry, called D'Almain, slain at Viterbo) et Dñi Ricardi Regis Roman. (Henry's father) iii. capellani divina celebrantes et præterea xii. scolares pauperes *secundarii* percipientes singuli vi. den. per Ebdom a xv*. S. Mich. usq. ad xv^m. S. Joann. Bapt. qui inter cæteros Eccles: obsequiis specialiter deputentur, et ad hanc sustentationem in forma de cæteris prænotata admittantur et ab eadem si meruerint expellantur."

This provision deserves remark not only for its historical import, as shewing that the close connection which existed between the founder and that very important personage, Richard, King of the Romans, passed on to his son, but as indicating an intention of having a second class of scholars, "secundarii," receiving a smaller allocation, and for only three quarters of the year. I believe that this intention was never carried out, but for what cause I am quite unable to state. A similar circumstance occurred in the neigh-

---

† This provision, which I believe to be quite singular, and arising out of the double location of the institution, was nevertheless continued in a modified form in the last statutes, and remained an effective practice for some centuries. In the earliest register of the college, 1482, a yearly *capitulum* is recorded as held in the manor of Holywell, as the most convenient centre, to which, after all the bailiffs had delivered their accounts, three questions were proposed:—1. "De mora et moribus custodis?" 2. "De statu maneriorum?" 3. (a financial consequence of No. 2), "Anne Numerus Sociorum augeri potest?" Pending the first inquiry the Warden resigned his keys, which were delivered to him again by the Sub-warden.

bouring estate of Barkby; the estate was conveyed in the following year, 1271 [a], by Robert, son of Peter de Percy, to the college [x], subject to the maintenance of three chaplains to celebrate for the souls of the whole royal family, but I know no evidence of this condition being observed.

The year 1272 was one of great political import to Walter de Merton. The patron whom he had so faithfully served through good and evil fortune, ended his long reign by a peaceful death, Nov. 16. This event, however, was the means of bringing the ex-Chancellor into greater prominence than before, and of proving how general was the confidence which he had won. The young king being absent on a crusade, a meeting of the principal nobles was held, which elected the Archbishop of York and the Earls of Cornwall and Gloucester guardians of the realm. The seal of the new monarch was delivered to Walter de Merton, and he found himself wielding an almost vice-regal power until the king's return. The writs issuing at this time under his hand, and still extant, are numerous. Many of them are transcribed by Kilner, who records that the latest he has found, dates July, 1274. (MS. note on Astrey's Life, p. 32.)

On Jan. 13 following, 1273, the Chancellor was recognised and formally constituted in his office by a convention of the estates at Westminster.

On the 9th of August, the king having reached Mellun on the Seine, wrote a letter of thanks to the Chancellor for his careful administration of the public affairs, with promise of ratifying all his acts. (Vid. Rym., *Fœd.*, tom. ii. p. 13.)

The king landed at Dover Aug. 2, 1274. The Chancellor must have resigned the seals immediately, for in his third and last body of statutes, issued in the same month, he describes himself as "quondam Cancellarius," and soon after, Sept. 21, his friend, Bishop Burnell of Bath and Wells, appears as his successor.

At this point ends his official connexion with the crown and state of England, and at the very same period commences his exaltation in the Church by election to the see of Rochester.

His election, which took place on the 20th of July, was confirmed on Oct. 21, and the same day he was consecrated by Arch-

---

[a] Final Concord, June, 1272; vid. Barkby Evidences, Merton Exch.

[x] The founder having paid him 160 marks of silver.

bishop Kilwardby, at Gillingham, near Rochester, the chapter of Rochester giving security that no prejudice should arise to the church of Canterbury by his being consecrated elsewhere [y].

We soon find him bestowing his bounty upon his new and ill-endowed dignity. He annexed [z] to his see the manors of Cole-hambury, and of Middleton Chenduit (now called Cheyney), in Northamptonshire, and he used his influence to enrich his attached and faithful employer, Peter de Abindon, the first Warden, by getting the abbey of Abingdon [a] to present him to the church of Newnham (Courtney), and by inducing Bishop Gravesend of Lincoln to allow him to hold the church *in commendam.*

The month of August, 1274, gave birth to the final body of statutes, which are still the authorized code for the government of the Merton scholars, except in so far as they are reversed or neutralized by the ordinance imposed by the Queen in Council under the University Reform Act of 1855.

It is remarkable that while he notices his late dignity of Chancellor, " quondam Cancellarius," he does not notice his approaching ecclesiastical elevation ; he was at this time bishop-elect.

The great change effected by these last statutes was not one of principle, but nevertheless one greatly enhancing the efficiency and perfectness of his institution, without which it never could have become the model of collegiate institutions.

It concentrated the divided members of the body in one home, and that in the University of Oxford, to which thenceforth it became permanently tied, and the " vel alibi, ubi Universitas viget studentium" was dropped.

"In eâ," i. e. the house adjoining St. John's Church, Oxford, " scolares *perpetuo* moraturos esse decerno," was his altered language, whilst he still willed them to bear their original title, " Domus scolarium de Merton," derived not from himself, but from his and their early connection with the priory of Merton.

His statutes were ratified by the new king, and thus carried the force of charter. He was allowed to insert in the clause conveying his property to his college not only certain specified manors, but also a prospective grant of future acquisitions, " una cum aliis per me sibi acquisitis aut acquirendis."

---

[y] Collect. MSS. Hen. Wharton, lib. notat. F. p. 77. .   [z] Annals of Edm. Hadenham. Anglia Sacra.   [a] Rot. Ric. Gravesend. A°. Pontificale 17°.

This license was one of remarkable width, especially when we consider that the grantor was a monarch remarkably jealous of the rapid amortizing which was then going on in his kingdom.

In 1275, March 29, the founder executed his will, in his favoured priory of Merton, and with the aid of the most august witnesses, Abp. Kilwardby of Canterbury, Bishop Burnell of Bath and Wells, (his successor in the chancellorship,) and the Pope's legate.

No document[b] can more fully reveal to us the founder's mind and heart than this most carefully-studied, considerate, just, and pious disposition of his vast worldly wealth. The statutes themselves, with all their repeated asseverations of gratitude to God as the Author of his prosperity, and of his desire to devote his substance to the great Giver's glory, do not so fully exhibit the deep reach of this principle as the minute provisions in his will.

In them he extends his consideration to the poor of every place whence his revenues accrued, to the carters and ploughmen of every manor which belonged to himself or his see, to numerous dependents by name. His attachment to places and kindred are also strongly revealed. His desire to be buried at Basingstoke with his parents; his bequest to his earliest eleemosynary creation, the humble hospital at Basingstoke; his bountiful care for those of his numerous kindred for whom he had not yet provided, are all evidences of a most loving and warmly-affectioned character, which we must admire the more for being unsullied by his long intermixture with politics and the rough statesmen and soldiers of his day.

In Lent, 1276, the Archbishop, Robert Kilwardby, held a visitation of the University of Oxford "jure metropolitano," attracted by various follies and errors which had crept into the schools[c], and by that prevailing corruption of grammar which had induced the founder of Merton to engraft a "grammaticus" upon his institution, to whom *all* the fellows, of whatever age, might have recourse, "absque rubore," for the amendment of the Latinity, which was prescribed for their common use, as their "idioma vulgare."

---

[b] See a full abstract and notes in the Appendix. Much as the will and executors' account have been studied, I commend them to more searching examination, in the confidence that it will elicit some new facts illustrative of the founder's history and of the persons connected with him. Vide Kilner's MSS., vol. i.

[c] A. Wood's *Hist. Acad. Oxon.* lib. i. pp. 125, 126; and Preface, p. 2.

To this visitation the college owes a double debt:—1. The settlement of the question of "patronus[d];" 2. The addition to the statutes of the Archbishop's interpretative ordinances, bearing the sanction of the founder's seal.

The character of these ordinances is very remarkable,—they are not corrective, but constructive, and that to the minutest detail of internal administration. It is difficult to conjecture any reason for the founder, with all his ample and practised powers of construction, invoking his friend's aid in putting the finishing touches to the details of his institution. We find the Archbishop appointing or ratifying the appointment by name of the first sub-warden, bursars, and deans. We find him regulating the bursarial periods, the weekly distribution of money for the fellows' commons, the monthly prospective estimate of the amount that could be afforded. He prescribes that the bursars shall keep the "munimenta" under three locks, and the books of the community under like safe-guard, to be assigned by warden and sub-warden to the fellows' uses, under sufficient pledge: that the seal be kept under five locks, and not used without the presence of five persons. He assigns to the three deans the duty of determining who and how many scholars are to live in each chamber; he gives them four marks per annum, and the bursars the same, in addition to the fifty received by every fellow, as his statutable allowance. He requires that every fellow shall leave his books to the college at death, or on entering a religious order. He legislates also for a body, not contemplated by the statutes, but created, I presume, by the straitness of the house of Merton, the "scolares extra domum agentes," and receiving their portions "de domo." These he requires to classify themselves according to the rate of their portions, so that they who receive 8d. a-week should live "in uno domicilio," and those who

---

[d] The early statutes nominate the Bishop of Winchester, as diocesan of Maldon, *patronus*. The removal of the *domus* to Oxford seems to have deprived him, in the founder's intention, of that relation to the college, but the intention is not expressed. A *patronus* is mentioned throughout the stat. 1274, but without any hint of its not being the Bishop of Winchester. The founder's rátification of Archbishop Kilwardby's ordinances must be taken as his ultimate determination. This is reiterated by Archbishop Pekham in 1284, and the reasons assigned, "quia Archiepiscopalis sublimior auctoritas, latior jurisdictio, zelus sincerior existere consuevit." These injunctions, for the sake of these reasons, Archbishop Parker ordered to be written in the Register of the college, when his authority was questioned in the matter of admitting Warden Mann.

·receive 6d. and 4d. likewise[e]. Finally, he ties the Masters of Arts to lecture for three years from their inception, and not to seek the Chancellor's license of inception without the cognizance of their college.

Whatever the cause which induced the founder to commit to his metropolitan so detailed an interference in his college, posterity has been a considerable gainer by the insight the ordinances have given into the interior of the Domus de·Merton, in its earliest stage of completed organization[f].

And now we come to the closing year of the founder's life, 1277. On Oct. 26th (Tuesday next before the feast of SS. Simon and Jude) he added a codicil to his will, making one material alteration, viz., the devising to his college the whole residue[g] of his personalty, instead of a fixed bequest of £1,000. On the 27th, the eve of SS. Simon and Jude, he died,—as his cotemporary[h] affirms, from the effects of a fall from his horse into a river which he was crossing. Others have added that the river was the Medway, and the place of his death Rochester. But it is clear that decay of life had set in long enough before death to give due forewarning, and to try remedial measures. The executors' payments[i] shew that the London faculty was invoked, "de London usque Soleby," but they leave us quite in the region of conjecture as to the locality[k] of the place in which the venerable patient lay. The submersion in the ford was then, most likely, antecedent to the fatal sickness, and. the addition of the codicil an indication of the patient's consciousness of the ebbing of his vital powers.

---

[e] Anxious to bring the "extrinseci" as much as possible into collegiate discipline, he adds,—" Custos aliquem de scholaribus suis assignet, qui dictis scholaribus in villa agentibus superintendat, ut per eum sciatur qualiter in moribus et literatura proficiant, et an eos ulterius sustentare expediat." Living "extra scolas" incurred immediate forfeiture of their portions. It appears, from an expression in this last clause, that these scholars were not members of the foundation,·but mere recipients of its temporary bounty. May they not be akin to the "secundarii" mentioned above as charged upon Kibworth manor ?

[f] See Archbishop Pekhàm's Injunctions, 1284, for a further insight into detail, and incipient corruption.

[g] By the will the residue was to be bestowed " in salutem animæ" by the executors aided by consultees.

[h] Thomas Wykes, living at Osney at this time. Vide Appendix.

[i] "v. marc Mᵣᵒ. Martino, Physico, pro salario suo per *multum* tempus et pro labore suo de London usque Soleby ante obitum episcopi."

[k] Evidently *not* in Hampshire, or he would have been buried at Basingstoke, according to his will.

He was honourably interred near the tomb of his predecessor, St. William, in the north wall of the north aisle, and nearly opposite to his throne. The executors' accounts[1] give us particulars of the sumptuous monument which arose over his remains, the chief peculiarity of which is its insertion in the thickness of the wall itself, beneath the sill of a window, and the insertion of new lights filled with coloured glass, just above the level of the monumental slab, and casting their chequered hues upon the inlaid brass of Limoges work. The whole expense of masonry, Limoges work, and iron railing, amounted to £70.

Within was laid the tall and portly body of the most munificent, probably the most able, statesman and prelate of the thirteenth century, habited in his bishop's robes, and accompanied by the sacred insignia of his office, the pastoral staff and chalice.

Twice, at intervals of nearly three centuries, he has been visited in his chamber of death. Once in the time of Sir Henry Savile's wardenship, 1598, once in our own day.

On the first occasion, the brass having been defaced by the reformers of Edward VI.'s reign, it was desired to replace the graven effigies of the founder and his simple inscription with sculptured effigies of alabaster, and with a lengthier inscription followed by a tetrastich. On removing the original slab, the body was found fully open to view; the staff, on being touched, fell to pieces, but the chalice, being sound, was removed to the college, and laid up in the "Cista Jocalium," the repository chest of all the college valuables.

The inscription given in the note[m] has little merit, except

---

[1] See Appendix, end of Will.

[m] "Walteri de Merton Cancellario
Angliæ sub Henr. III.; Ep'o
Roffensi sub Edv. I.; Re, Unius
Exemplo, omnium quotquot extant
Collegiorum, Fundatori; Maximorum
Europæ Totius Ingeniorum Felicissimo
Parenti; Custos et Scholl. Domus
Scholarium de Mert. in Univ. Oxon.
Communibus Coll. Impensis Monumento posuere."
"A.D. 1598.   H. Savile, Custode."

"Ob. in Vigiliâ Simonis et Judæ. A.D. 1277. Ed. I. v°."

"Inchoaverat Coll. Maldoniæ in Agro Surr., A.D. 1264. Hen. III. xlviii°., cui dein Salubri Consilio Oxonium A°. 1270 translato, Extrema Manus felicissimis, ut credi par est, auspiciis accessit, A°. 1274, ipsis Kal. Augusti. A°. R. R. Ed. I. ii°."

for the one terse and very true expression, " Re, unius; exemplo omnium, quotquot extant collegiorum, fundator." It seems to deny his chancellorship under Edward I., and is calculated to mislead as to the Oxford connection of the college from its first existence, and as to the exact time of the concentration of its detached members, on which point probably Warden Savile was actually misinformed.

When, then, in the year 1852 the college was strongly urged, by the decayed condition of the tomb, to undertake a complete re-newal, it was resolved not to replace the inscription or the sculp-ture, but to follow as nearly as possible the details of the original work, which the executors' accounts happily supplied.

The sculptured effigies were then removed, and in the presence of deputed members, both of the chapter and of the college, the honoured remains were again laid bare: the skeleton was found to measure six feet, even in its decay; the fragments of the staff and of the cloth of gold were still discernible, but no other relic, not even a ring[n]. A new slab was immediately laid over the re-mains, with the earnest hope that at least three centuries might pass again before any need should arise for disturbing the honoured sepulchre; a brass, inlaid with colour, and cut with a simple legend of name, titles, and date, was fixed in the slab; the windows were re-opened and filled with stained glass, and a protective iron railing of suitable character erected in front.

" Magne Senex titulis, Musarum Sede sacrata
    Major, Mertonidum maxime Progenie:
  Hæc tibi gratantes post sæcula sera Nepotes
  En votiva locant marmora, sancte Parens."

Another tablet was added in 1662, in the wardenship of Sir Thomas Clayton, to record the repair of the tomb after the damage done by the "rabies fanaticorum." This tablet was so unhappily placed as to block up the small windows, which were pro-posed by the designer of the tomb to throw a coloured light upon the slab and its engraved and enamelled brass.

It may here be added, that the chalice was used by the Cavalier members of the college, at the time of the Rebellion and after, as a drinking-cup, and destroyed. MS. A. Wood, quoted by Kilner, *Pythagoras*, p. 54.

[n] This probably was removed at the time of the removal of the chalice, but no ac-count of its fate is extant. A massive gold ring, engraved with a three-quarter figure bearing a palm-branch, and surrounded by the motto, " Qui timet Dominum, faciet bona," was left by the late Warden Berdmore to the Compton family, and is now worn by the Rev. Berdmore Compton, late fellow of Merton, but of its past history nothing is known. The founder's signet-ring was certainly of this device, which may be seen in several seals now in the College Exchequer, or in Kilner's engraving at the end of his *Pythagoras*.

It may be remarked that this tomb, sumptuous as it was for its day, and adequate to its object, is strikingly differenced from those far more sumptuous erections which arose in the succeeding centuries over the remains of succeeding founders, such as Chichèley, Wykeham, and Waynfleet.   Merton's tomb is simply a monument; the latter are not only monuments, they are also chapels or chantries for obituary services, furnished with altars and shrines, and leaving room for the ministrations of a priest.   They exhibit the growth of that ardent desire for propitiatory offices after death, which went on growing till the time of the Dissolution, and to which, undoubtedly, we owe a very large proportion of the benefactions of the mediæval centuries, and of many of the architectural adornments which still are the glory of our land.   Walter de Merton was not by any means free from the idea of benefiting the departed soul, in its purgatorial state, by the purchased prayers of beneficiaries, for he left, by his first will, his whole residue, *in salutem animæ*, and provided chaplains to celebrate for his own and his parents' benefit; but he seems to have held this idea in a sober subordination to the higher motives (so plainly published in the preamble of his statutes) of glorifying God by his works of charity, and making a grateful return to the Giver of all good; and I cannot but regard his monument (for which, it may be remarked, he cared to leave no special provision) as in some measure an evidence of the truth of those words of his which are meant to declare his dominant motives in the disposition of his worldly wealth:—"De summi rerum et bonorum opificis bonitate confisus. . . .   Ejusdem gratiæ, qui vota hominum pro sua voluntate disponit et dirigit, fidenter innisus. . . . Si quid sui nominis honori aliquid retribuam, sæpe solicitus."— *Statutes*, 1274.

And these words and these motives I cannot do better than commend to the pious consideration and the loving imitation of all who bear his name, or profit by his benefactions.

APPENDIX.

DOCUMENTS ILLUSTRATIVE OF THE SKETCH OF WALTER DE MERTON'S LIFE.

1. An abstract of his will, with extracts from the executors' accounts.
2. The founder's character, as described in the Hexameters of Thomas Wykes, a Canon of Osney, and chronicler of his own times, who must frequently have seen the founder during his residences in Oxford with the court.
3. A pedigree, shewing the issue of the founder's sisters, and the relationship to him of many of his legatees, and of several of the early members of the college.

WILL OF WALTER DE MERTON.
(Printed *in extenso* by Kilner, Suppl., p. 82.)

This document is very interesting, not only from its antiquity, importance of the testator, and the great amount of property conveyed, but from the picture which it gives of the testator's mind, especially of its tenderness, piety, and comprehensiveness, exhibited in his detailed consideration of the claims of his kindred, of his dependents, of the places whence his wealth accrued, and of his eleemosynary children.

The will is found in Abp. Peckham's Register, fo. 103. 3.

Executed at Merton, March, 1275-6.

Codicil added, Oct., 1277.

Final audit of executors' account, May, 1282.

The *Compotus Executorum* and the *Petitiones super Executoribus* are still extant with the will, and are interesting documents.

Witnesses who attached their seals besides seven others named..........
{ Archbishop (Kilwardby) of Canterbury.
Bishop (Burnell) of Bath and Wells, Lord Chancellor.
The Pope's nuncio, Roger de Nogeriis.

Executors. William de Ewell; John de Merston and Friar Thomas de Woldeham (his chaplains); John de Catteloyn; Ralph de Riplingham; William Dodekin; Ranulph, vicar of Greenwich, added by codicil.

Councillors to the Executors[a].—Bishop of Bath and Wells; John de Kerkeby, Justiciar 1233, Bishop of Ely 1286; Andrew de Kirkenny.

Directions about Burial.—If he should die[b] in co. Hants., to be buried in Basingstoke Church with his parents. If elsewhere, in Rochester Cathedral.

BEQUESTS.

1. *For Masses.*—To Basingstoke Church a chalice, pret. 5 mks.; for five chaplains celebrating for one year in that church, or neighbouring ones, or at Oxford, if "idonei" not to be found on the spot, 25½ mks.

2. *At Rochester.*—For five chaplains celebrating one year, 25½ mks. To his successor[c], his mitre, staff, and one of his rings. To his chapter, for purchase of some estate for celebration of an *obit* and a distribution of bread to the poor, 100 mks. To the prior, one of his palfreys and a silver cup. To the works of the cathedral, 10 mks.

3. *To Parishes where he held Preferment.*—Poor of Stayndrop, 20 mks. Sedgefield, 40 mks. Hautwyse[d], 25 mks. Codington[e], 20 mks. Bernyngham[f], 10 mks., with 100s. *ad ornamenta ecclesiæ.* Braunceton[g], 15 mks. Fynsbury[h], 40s. Prebend. of Sarum:—Bere, 18 mks.; Charminster, 12 mks.

4. *To Religious Houses.*—Tortington[i], Sussex, 40s. Friers Minors[k] in Oxford, 25 mks.; London, 25 mks.; Hartlepool, 10 mks.; Friers Preachers in Oxford, 10 mks.; Newcastle-on-Tyne, 10 mks.: the glossed Epistles

---

[a] These probably were needed on account of the provision in the will that the residue should be applied "ad salutem animæ." The codicil relieved the executors of this delicate duty by giving the residue to the college.

[b] This was evidently his humble wish, "si hoc mihi misericordia Dei concedat."

[c] In the petitions, his successor, not contented with these bequests, "petit 1. capellam? integram pret. xx. m. quam Eccl. Roff. de consuetudine debet habere a mortuo Epo;" and for dilapidations of houses and stock, £60.

Also the executors paid to the precentor, as his right, 30s. for making a roll to carry through England, "memoriam obitus Epi defuncti."

The Rochester accounts were very complicated, Walter's claims on the estate of his predecessor, Laurence, being still unsatisfied, and several of the dignitaries being in debt to their bishop.

[d] Supposed to be Haltwhistle, Northumberland, in the patronage of the Bishop of Durham. No evidence exists, except this bequest, of the founder having held the rectory.

[e] In Surrey, adjoining Maldon. Appropriated 2 Edw. II. to Merton Priory. Walter de Portsmue, his nephew, was rector at the founder's death.

[f] In the deanery of Richmond, Yorkshire. Crown patronage.

[g] In Lincolnshire. Will. de Ewell, his nephew, succeeded him in 1272.

[h] Prebend in St. Paul's Cathedral.

[i] From whence he obtained the advowson of Farleigh.

[k] With these three bodies of Franciscans and the two Dominican houses he was brought into contact by his preferments in London and Durham and his sojournings in Oxford with the court, which must have been frequent.

of St. Paul to be restored to them.   Nuns of St. Helen[1], London, 100s.
Nuns of Wyntneye[m], 40s.

5. *His Kindred*[n].—His sister de Wortyng, 30 mks.

To her unmarried daughter, to marry her, or otherwise provide neces-
saries, 30 mks.

His sister Edith, to buy land, or otherwise provide security, besides the
lands he bought for her, 80 mks.

To her eldest son, to buy land, or otherwise, 30 mks.

To her daughter at Wilton (nunnery), to provide more fully for her
clothing and diet in the house, 20 mks.

To his sister Agnes, 20 mks.

To Alan de Portesmue, to buy lands, 60 mks.

To Hugh Chastayn, Littlemilne Mill, 5 mks.

To Thomas, his brother, 40 mks.

To Thomas de la Dune[o], 5 mks.

To John Jakelin and wife, "quæ eis secretius liberentur," 10 mks.

To Plesentia de London, 10 mks.

To Hawise, her sister, 10 mks.

To Alan de Langford and wife, 10 mks.

To John le Coppe, 4 mks.

To Nicolas de Theddene, and wife and boys, 30 mks.

To John de Sandeford and wife, 100s.

6. *To Friends and Dependents.*

To Master Peter[p] de Abendon, (first warden), one of his palfreys and silver cup.

To Master Andrew[q], offic.? silver cup and 40 mks.

---

[1] Near Finsbury.

[m] Hartley Wintney, near Basingstoke.

[n] See the pedigree, and therein notice that those provided for in his foundation are not provided for in the will.

[o] Married his niece Edith. See Rot. Claus. 2 Edw. I. m. 14. Receipt from Thomas for 100 marks "de maritagio neptis Waltero," 1273, feast of St. Lucy. She was to re-main in her uncle's guardianship till Easter, "de curialitate suâ," and then to go to her husband's home.

[p] Had been in charge of the "scholares" from their earliest institution, *circa* 1262. He claims from the executors *nomine proprio* £100, for his labours and costs during seventeen years and more in the Lord Walter's service, and in name of the college sums exceeding £800, which the founder had received from Eleham, Ponteland, Stilling-ton, Seton, and elsewhere. It would appear that the founder still acted as receiver of those estates, which lay in convenient nearness to his own agents. As Rector of Sedge-field, &c., he was still deriving a revenue from Durham, and as Bishop of Rochester he was obliged to have bailiffs who could easily visit Eleham, near Canterbury. The be-quest of the residue was probably intended to cover all this debt to his college.

[q] The same as Andrew de Kirkenny, often written Kilkenny, present at the Bishop's death. Probably his official principal.

To John Cateloyn[r] (an executor), 40 mks.

To William Sarum, silver cup and 5 mks.

To Wm. Dodekin (an executor), 100 mks.

To John de Merston, chaplain, 50 mks.

To Robert Fitz-Nigel[s] all the interest he had in his lands; and towards the restoring of them 30 mks.

To Roger Taylard, besides the 5 mks. life-rent-charge he had at Kybworth, 40 mks.

To Will. de Mertock, 15 mks.

To Will. de Saddeburgh[t] (Sedburgh), 40 mks., and remittance of his debt for tithes at Butterwyk.

To John de Stanhope, 20 mks.

To Peter the Clerk, 40s.

To John } Cook[u] { 30 mks.
To Walter }   { 20 mks.

To John de Kancia[v], 5 mks.

To Henry de Elham, 10 mks.

To John Hydeys, 100s.

To Hugh de Borstall, 100s.

To Adam Sauveage, 100s.

To William Prepositus[x] of Bromlegh, 40s.

To Adam de la Wytheyenbiry[y], 20s.

To Peter and John Baker, (by trade or surname?) a lease at Bere.

To Peter Marshall, 60s.

To Philip of Dertford, 50s.

To Peter the Cook, 40s.

To Henry the Cook, 10s.

To Simon, 20s.

To John the Taylor, 20s.

To William Watteso, 40s.

To Thomas Catel, 100s.

To Adam the Palfreyman[z], 40s.

To John de Mersham, 2 mks.

To John Makeney, 2 mks.

To Geoffrey the Carter, 2 mks.

To Elias Page, 40s.

To William Wodegate, 1 mk.

To Robert de Chetyndon, 20s.

To Richard the Carter, 20s.

To Walter the Carter, double stipend for the year of Testator's death.

To the other carters and ploughmen in each manor, besides their stipend[a], 5s.

Total, £16 5s.

---

[r] An old retainer; claims of the executors £40 for sixteen years' service in various places, "tam in curia regis quam extra cum opus fuit in negotiis Dni W."

[s] Married a niece. See Rot. Chart. 49 Henry III. m. 2. A grant to Walter of Robert's lands, confiscated by his joining the Earl of Leicester. This grant was probably obtained by the founder as a friendly arrangement. The executors paid the Countess of Winchester 20 marks for harbouring Robert's wife, (no doubt at the time of his attainder); to William St. John, who married his sister, for dowry promised, £30; to the Abbess of Ambresbury, for another sister, 12 marks, promised on her being veiled in that house; and to Robert himself 100 marks, promised by the founder in tempore mortis.

[t] This and the following name shew how he kept up his connection with the North.

[u] Cocus, I think, stands here for a surname. It occurs in the Basingstoke evidences. Peter Cocus, below, I assume to be a servant, from the amount assigned.

[v] A Basingstoke name.

[x] A name commonly given in the Bailiff's Rolls of the college to the head bailiff of a manor. Bromley was a chief manor of the see of Rochester.

[y] See below. The estate to be sold "in subsidium terræ sanctæ."

[z] Palfridarius, a common word for groom.

[a] On this account the executors paid 325s. to sixty-five persons on fourteen manors.

7. *Other Friends.*

To Philip de Codinton (a kinsman), 15 mks.

To William de Grafton[b], the next crops of Wolveton farm, (value £10 15s.,) and 10 mks.

To Gerard the Chaplain, 5 mks.

To Richard de Bradmere, 40s.

To William de Osemundleye, 1 mk.

To William de Haketon, 40s.

To Richard Russel, 10 mks.

To William the Cook[c], who is at Osney, 1 mk.

To Robert de Waltham, 100s.

To Roger Bidhey, 20s.

To William the Carter, 10s.

To the mother of Alan of Langford, 4 mks.

To John de Watevile[d], 40 mks.

To Thomas the Forester, 50s.

To Richard de la Hoke, 20s.

To the daughter of Dulcia of Maldon, 100s.

To the sister of John de Farnham and her husband, 30 mks.

To the mother of Walter of Odyham, a silver cup.

To the wife of the late Peter de Codinton, 40s.

To Robert de Creuker, unless otherwise settled with him, 10 mks.

To Saer de Harcourt[e], 10 mks.

To provide for two daughters of Lord[f] Stephen Chenduit, in marriage or otherwise, 80 mks. If less will do, the surplus to provide similarly for other daughters.

To Stephen's wife, 20 mks.

8. *To the College.* — To buy land in perpetuity, unless needed "pro defensione jurium," 1,000 mks. (*solutæ.*)

9. *To Basingstoke Hospital.* — To buy land, and no other purpose, 450 mks.[g]

For a chaplain perpetually celebrating there, 100 mks.

If purchase cannot be made in four years, college to take the money, and pay £20 annually to hospital; or if college decline the charge, to be entrusted to some religious house.

10. *The Holy Land.*—Lease of Wythenbery to be sold, and proceeds

---

[b] He claims of executors, as "clericus cancellariæ qui fuit cum Epo defuncto," 38 mks., laid out by the Bishop's order on the church of Blecchesworth, (near Dorking ?).

[c] All notes of connection with Osney are worth remark, as strengthening the tradition that the founder resided there during his academical course, and as adding to the doggrel lines of Thomas Wykes, the Osney canon, the value of an eye-witness's description. See below, "the Osney missal to be restored."

[d] Of the Watevile family, who were mesne lords of Maldon.

[e] From whom he obtained the manor of Kibworth Harcourt, Leicestershire.

[f] From whom, as mesne lord, he obtained the manors of Cuxham, Oxon, Chetindon, Bucks., and Middleton Cheney, (i. e. Chenduit,) Northants. Both these lords were, like a great number of the landowners at the end of Henry the Third's baronial wars, in the hands of Jew money-lenders. The college still possesses the acquittances from the Jews on being paid off by the founder, whose purse came to the relief of the mortgagors in these two cases, as in the case of the Wateviles, mesne lords of Malden, the Leicesters, lords of Gamlingay, and the Fitz-Eustaces, lords of the Cambridge manors.

[g] In 1280 Peter Abindon, Warden, bought several parcels of land at Basingstoke and Ywode. Vid. Pat. Rot. 12 Ed. I. m. 17.

applied to sending some good man "in subsidium terræ sanctæ, pro me et seipso."

11. *The King.*—His best silver cup [h] and cover, and pair of silver dishes.

12. *Other Single Bequests.*—To Lord Antony Bek[i], my best ring, and my houses at Sarum; or if he declines them, to my nephew Will. de Ewell, who shall keep them up for Antony's use whenever he pleases.

To the Lord John de Kirkeby, a gold ring, a mazer cup, and silver cup.

To Master Roger de Seyton, a ring, and his silver scultella for alms.

To the Lord John de Kobham, a ring.

To Walter de Odyam, a silver cup and two silver scultellæ.

To Master William de Ewell, his Bible (price 4 mks.), with remainder to the scholars, and the mazer cup at Sedgefield.

Also to Will., out of the income of Sedgefield, for each year since his consecration, £100, and to John de la Clyve, nephew, £5, besides silver vessels.

To Master Reymund, a silver cup.

To Ralph Riplyngham[k] (an executor), 30 mks.

To Abbot of Osney, the missal to be restored.

In case the estate should fail to pay all the above bequests, his sisters' families, his college, William Dudekyn, John and Walter Cook, were to have their portions in full.

The residue to be applied "in salutem animæ," at executors' discretion.

Total bequeathed in money, £2,014 17s. 0d.
Articles valued . . . . 711 8s. 6d.

Total . . . £2,726 5s. 6d.

Codicil.—Thursday before feast of SS. Simon and Jude, 1277, (on the eve of which feast he died.)

The ploughs on two episcopal manors to go with the see.

Ralph, vicar of Greenwich, added to his executors.

---

[h] Prynne Records, tom. ii. p. 384. The king, by custom, claimed the palfrey and cup of every bishop deceased. See Claus. Rot., 39 Hen. III., in dorso, "De Palfrido Abbatis de Osneye."
In Anglia Sac., i. p. 88, the archbishop is said to have right to the palfrey, cup, seals, and dogs of a bishop of Rochester, and the king only by vacancy of the archbishopric.

[i] Antony and Thomas, sons of the Baron Bek, of Grimsthorp, Lincolnshire, were resident in a house (on the site of the college) bought by the founder in 1266 of a Jew, who bargained for their being allowed to remain for three years. They were receiving their academical education, and were probably taken as commoners into the new house of scholars. Antony seems to have won the founder's favour. He became Bishop of Durham 1283—1311, and Patriarch of Jerusalem. He was commonly known as the "Fighting Bishop."

[k] Called Garderobarius in the Comp. Exec., where he claims 40s. for a horse that died at the funeral, and for making the inventory.

Bequests to legatees deceased to go to their friends.

Residue to the college.

Warden, Peter de Abindon was appointed auditor, probably as representing the college, the largest legatee, and his largest creditor. The executors' accounts were audited in the chapel of the chancery of St. Paul's, London, but not till 4½ years after the decease[1], May, 1282. The property in both provinces, Canterbury and York, was brought to one account. Amongst the executors' payments worth noting occur:—

"v. marc M^ro. Martino Physico pro salario suo per multum temp. et pro labore suo de London usq. Soleby^m, ante obitum epi.

"v^s. vii^d. Hen. de la More Aurifabro pro confectione annulorum et reparacione Cyphorum.

"xl^li. v^s. vi^d. Liberat. Magistro Johanni Burgensi Limovicensi pro tumba dni episcopi Roffensis, scilicet pro constructione et cariagio de Lymoges usque Roffam.

"Et xlvi^s. viii^d. Cuidam executori eunti apud Lymoges ad ordinandam & providendam constructionem dictæ tumbæ.

"Et x^s. viii^d. Cuidam garcioni eunti apud Lymoges, querenti dictam tumbam constructam & ducenti eam cum dicto magistro usque Roffam.

"Et xxii^li. in maceoneria circa dictam tumbam defuncti.

"Et vii. marcas in ferramento ejusdem, et cariagio ejusdem a Lond. usque Roffam, et aliis parandis ad dictam tumbam [iv^li. xiii^s. iv^d.]

"Et xi^s. Cuidam vitriario pro vitrio fenestrarum juxta tumbam dni Episcopi, apud Roffam."—Summa, lxx^li. vii^s. ii^d.

II.

"A°. 1274, Dominus Walter de Merton consecratus est in episcopum Roffensem; vir magnificus et secularis sapientie admodum eruditus: hic semper fuit, viris religiosis super omnia in suis negotiis promovendis, promptissimus adjutor et promotor.

"Eodem anno, [anno 1277,] in vigilia apostolorum Symonis et Jude, obiit Walterus de Merton, episcopus Roffensis, de cujus moribus quidam versificator dixit, [himself probably]:—

"Presul Walterus Roffensis pontificali
Culmine sincerus, virtute micans speciali,
Qui de Mertona vulgari more vocatus,
Cujus fama bona, gestus super omnia gratus,
Fidus in alloquio, justus, sermone modestus,
Cautus consilio, castus, socialis, honestus.
Dilexit clerum, gratis tribuens alimentum:
Pro quo Walterum benedicit turma studentum.
Oxonie studium per eum quasi plantula vernat,
Conferat auxilium sibi Rex qui cuncta gubernat."

---

[1] Still were not complete. In Madox's "Exchequer," c. 2. x., the Earl Marshal (Roger Bigot) acknowledged his debt of £60 to the Bishop of Rochester's executors. Recogn. in Scaccario, 17 Edw. I. fin. 1289.

^m Where? The founder is supposed to have died somewhere not far from Rochester.

PEDIGREE OF WALTER DE MERTON'S COLLATERALS.

(Taken chiefly from three Returns of the Founder's Kin, made about ten years after his death, penes Coll. Mert.)

N.B. Six coheirs found at the *Inquisitio Post Mortem*, marked 6.
The first eight *scolares*, marked 8.
Legatees marked L

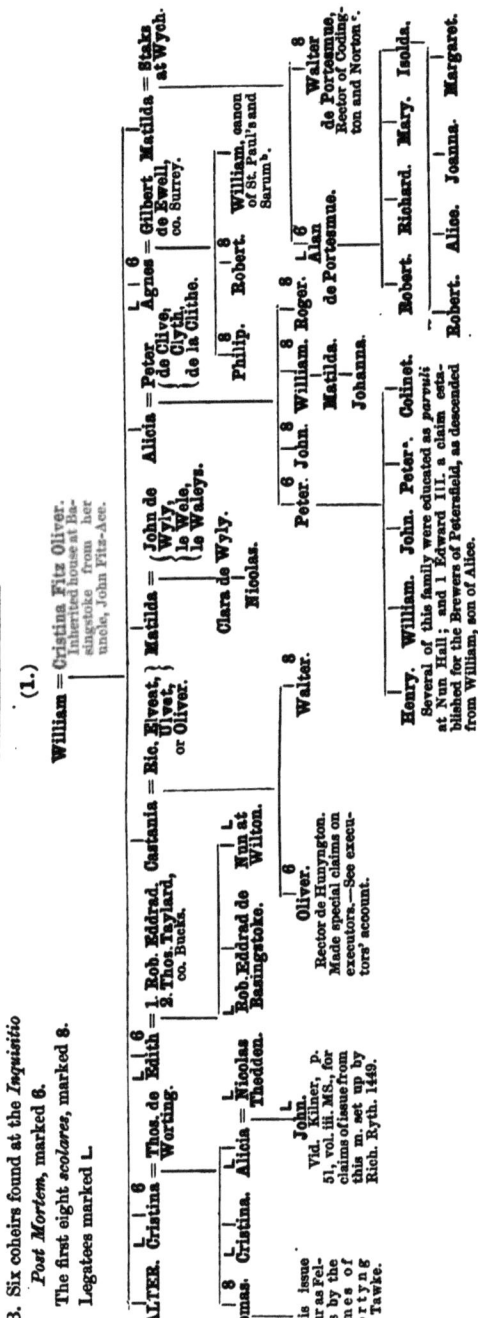

[a] 2 Edw. III. renounces his claim on Coll. for pension of 5 mks. : '*dummodo clericaliter vixerit.*' [b] The principal executor and large legatee. Rector of Braunceton on his uncle's resignation. [c] Some of this family probably bore the name of Codington.

Besides those named here, there were others called nieces and nephews :—
Edith, married to Thomas de la Dune, with a portion of 100 marks, given by her uncle. See Kilner, vol. i. MS. App.
Philip de Dertford, a legatee, called *nepos*.
Robert fil. Nigelli, or Fitz Neale, married a niece. See Will.

(2.)

CHASTAYNE, OR KYNGSMYLLE.

Margaret Fitz Oliver = William Chastayne de Kyngsmylle.
(sister of founder's mother.)

- **Richard Bysshop,** *de quo erat exitus.*
  - **William,** *qui ivit in Terram Sanctam;* probably by aid of bequest left in founder's will for sending a *vir bonus* to the Crusades.
    - **Hugo.**
    - **William,** *dictus de la Kingesmylle.*
      - **Thomas,** *qui est in Cantia.*
      - **William Bysshop.**
    - **Thomas.**
      - **Will.**
      - **Joh. Clericus.**
        - **Thom.**
      - **Rad.**
      - **Juliana.**
- **Emma,** *unde* Adam de Petersfield, (a Fellow).
- **Castania.**
  - **Agnes.** John de Say.
- **Alicia.**
  - **Joannes Bernard de Ywood.**
    - **Thomas.**
- **Christina de Ewell.**
  - **William.**
  - **Johanna,** *et alii.*

(3.)

Walter Fitz Oliver = Emma.
(founder's grandfather.)

Robert Fitz Oliver =
(founder's uncle.)

- **John le Gamene.**
  - **John.**
- **Alicia.**
- **Goda.**
- **Matilda.**
- **Joanna.**
  - **Robert,**
  - **Dominicus,**
  - **John,**
  - **William,**
  - **Alicia,**

Of this stock came Bernards (2), Dollrype, Yardley, Lee, and Sheffelde, all Fellows in time of Edward III., Henry VI., and Edward IV.

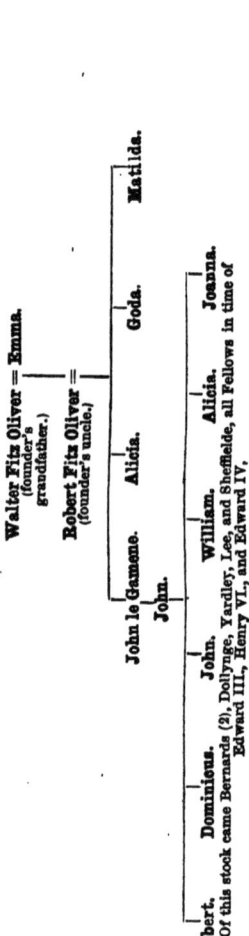

(2.)

CHASTAYNE, OR KYNGSMYLLE.

Margaret Fitz Oliver = **William Chastayne de Kyngsmylle.**
(sister of founder's mother.)

William, *qui ivit in Terram Sanctam;* probably by aid of bequest left in founder's will for sending a *vir bonus* to the Crusades. — **Richard Bysshop,** *de quo erat exitus.* — **Emma,** *uxor* Adam de Petersfield (a Fellow). — **Castania.** — **Agnes.** John de Say. — **Alicia.** Joannes Bernard de Ywood. — **Christina de Ewell.**

Hugo. — **William,** *dictus de la Kyngesmylle.* — **Thomas.** — **Juliana.**

Thomas, *qui est in Cantia.* — **William Bysshop.** — **Bad'.**

Will. — Joh. Clericus. — Thom.

Thomas. — William. — Johanna, *et alii.*

(3.)

Walter Fitz Oliver = **Emma.**
(founder's grandfather.)

Robert Fitz Oliver =
(founder's uncle.)

John le Gaumme. — **Alicia.** — **Goda.** — **Matilda.**

John.

Robert. — Dominicus. — John. — William. — Alicia. — Joanna.

Of this stock came Bernards (2), Dollynge, Yardley, Lee, and Sheffelde, all Fellows in time of Edward III., Henry VI., and Edward IV.